KU-792-544

Born and raised on the Wirral Peninsula, in England, **Charlotte Hawkes** is mum to two intrepid boys who love her to play building block games with them and who object loudly to the amount of time she spends on the computer. When she isn't writing—or building with blocks—she is company director for a small Anglo/French construction company. Charlotte loves to hear from readers, and you can contact her at her website: charlotte-hawkes.com.

Also by Charlotte Hawkes

The Army Doc's Secret Wife
The Surgeon's Baby Surprise

Hot Army Docs miniseries

Encounter with a Commanding Officer
Tempted by Dr Off-Limits

Discover more at millsandboon.co.uk.

TEMPTED BY DR OFF-LIMITS

CHARLOTTE HAWKES

MILLS & BOON

All rights reserved including the right of reproduction in whole or in part in any form. This edition is published by arrangement with Harlequin Books S.A.

This is a work of fiction. Names, characters, places, locations and incidents are purely fictional and bear no relationship to any real life individuals, living or dead, or to any actual places, business establishments, locations, events or incidents. Any resemblance is entirely coincidental.

This book is sold subject to the condition that it shall not, by way of trade or otherwise, be lent, resold, hired out or otherwise circulated without the prior consent of the publisher in any form of binding or cover other than that in which it is published and without a similar condition including this condition being imposed on the subsequent purchaser.

® and TM are trademarks owned and used by the trademark owner and/or its licensee. Trademarks marked with ® are registered with the United Kingdom Patent Office and/or the Office for Harmonisation in the Internal Market and in other countries.

First published in Great Britain 2017
by Mills & Boon, an imprint of HarperCollins*Publishers*
1 London Bridge Street, London, SE1 9GF

Large Print edition 2018

© 2017 Charlotte Hawkes

ISBN: 978-0-263-07286-0

MIX
Paper from
responsible sources
FSC C007454

This book is produced from independently certified FSC™ paper to ensure responsible forest management. For more information visit www.harpercollins.co.uk/green.

Printed and bound in Great Britain
by CPI Group (UK) Ltd, Croydon, CR0 4YY

Montgomery and Bartholomew,
my beautiful boys.
Make every step one you believe in and shine.
xxx

CHAPTER ONE

'HEY, GORGEOUS, THOSE lips of yours look so lonely, do they wanna meet mine?'

It took Elle a moment to realise the cheesy pick-up line had been aimed—or, more accurately, *slurred*—at her. She cringed and hoped that if she ignored him he might get the message, even as a part of her wondered why she didn't make one of the witty, no-nonsense comebacks for which she was renowned among her army colleagues.

Two weeks ago she would have.

In fact, two weeks ago she wouldn't have been sitting on this barstool, having nursed the same warm drink for the last couple of hours. She'd have been tearing up that dance-floor, alone or not.

Then again, two weeks ago she hadn't walked in on her fiancé, Stevie, in bed with not one—as she'd told her best friend, Fliss, in some last desperate grasp at dignity—but two bimbos. Two. As if cheating on her wasn't enough, he had to utterly humiliate her. They were football groupies, who'd then sold their sordid selfies to the tabloids. And in that moment it had been as though Stevie had stripped away all of Elle's self-assurance, the very foundation of her confidence, which had been so carefully cultivated over the last decade or so, leaving her feeling more like the nerdy, geeky outsider of her youth.

The fifteen-year-old girl who had let her new stepmother bully her when her bereaved father hadn't been around, and her schoolmate peers had pushed her around when her adored teachers hadn't been looking, until the cool, sixteen-year-old rising football star Stevie had taken a shine to her and everyone had reluctantly backed off. They hadn't disappeared altogether but had hovered, waiting for their chance to pounce as soon as Stevie dumped her.

But he hadn't, they'd been together for fifteen years in total. Two kids from a no-shoes-poor background who had dreamed of breaking free. He was the only boy she'd ever kissed, the only man she'd ever slept with. Without his support—both emotional and financial—her deep-seated desire of going to university to study medicine would have remained a pipe dream.

She was only grateful that her photo hadn't appeared within Stevie's double-page spread, including the moment he'd scored the winning goal for his club in the most recent Premier League match. *And surely that in itself was fairly damning?* Her photo hadn't been there because—fifteen years or not—the press had, mercifully, never really known about her. For the first few years of their relationship they'd been practically inseparable, looking for each other in school or at lunch-breaks, and then she'd gone to university and everything had changed. For almost the last decade of her relationship with Stevie she'd tried to keep her life and career as a respected army trauma doctor as far away from his professional footballer lifestyle as she possibly could.

'*Man*, what's a bloke gotta do t'get some attention around here?'

Elle startled as the drunk man next to her lolled over the bar, trying in vain to get the bartender to notice him. She refrained from telling him that she'd seen sober people wait up to about ten minutes to get served; she doubted he'd get anything more to drink from anyone. He seemed to have forgotten about her and she didn't particularly want to engage the bloke when she didn't have to.

She glanced around the bar-cum-club with its Latin dance vibe and sexily dressed patrons and reminded herself why she'd come tonight. In a matter of days she'd be thousands of miles away back on the second half of her latest tour of duty, and after the last fortnight holed up in her hotel room down the road she'd had something of a light-bulb moment. Why was she letting someone else—why she was letting *Stevie*—control her happiness, when it finally occurred to her that aside from the shock and humiliation of walking in on…*that*, she wasn't remotely as devastated as she perhaps should feel. If anything, a tiny part of her actually thought it felt…*relief*? So she'd ended up here, trying to be cool and independent and remind herself of the strong, capable woman she'd finally become, instead of the insecure, frightened girl she'd felt on discovering her fiancé's betrayal.

Instead, she just felt like a fish so far out of water she might as well have been back in the scorching desert she knew so well. It was time for her to cut her losses and go back to her hotel room, indulge in a long soak and snuggle down into that huge, fluffy, pure white bed. In a couple of days she'd be back out on her tour of duty and back into an environment she understood. Some people hated their jobs, but she loved hers. Always had. A small smile of relief tugged at her mouth.

'You took your time, huh, darlin', but I guess your lips liked the idea of meeting mine after all?'

Elle barely had time to snap back to reality to realise that the drunk man was still there, and was now lurching towards her with an excited gleam in his eye, clearly taking it as an invitation to plant a sloppy wet one on her. Apparently ignoring him hadn't worked after all, and now a second guy hovered in the background, grinning inanely at his buddy's apparent good fortune.

'Like I said…' she pulled away hastily, but caught off guard she was barely able to keep herself from toppling backwards off her barstool '…I'm not interested.'

'Sure you are, hot stuff. You just don't know it yet.'

A grabby hand snagged hers and she had to yank sharply to free it, her attitude changing immediately as she pulled herself back together.

'You're not listening,' Elle ground out coldly. 'I'm *really* not interested.'

'Tell you what…' he leered like he was making some huge concession '…I'll even buy you a drink to help loosen you up.'

'You're not the first man—and I use that term loosely where you're concerned—to offer to buy me a drink this evening and I declined.' A few of them had been pretty good looking, too, and she still hadn't been tempted. 'They were polite about it and took no for an answer. I suggest you do the same.'

If she had to physically defend herself, she knew she could. The army had trained her well enough, even though she'd been fortunate enough never to have to use it in practice. But it didn't mean her stomach wasn't churning in a way that it hadn't been a moment ago, or that she preferred not to make her debut in a bar back in the UK with some inebriated idiot.

'Aw, c'mon, don't be a tease…'

Elle reacted, some of her old self racing back to her in that instant as her hand closed swiftly, efficiently and discreetly over his, exerting just enough pressure on the first joint of his thumb. The words suddenly died on the man's lips, replaced with an audible intake of breath while his eyes bulged slightly. She felt a sliver of pride slip back into place.

Abruptly she became aware of someone stepping up behind her. Her grip still firm, Elle was about to turn around when the look on the drunk man's face changed as his bloodshot eyes attempted to focus just to the right of Elle's shoulder and upwards. And then up again. He clearly didn't like what he saw and she could only assume it was someone coming to her rescue.

Not that she needed rescuing. Stevie might have knocked her confidence as a woman, but he certainly hadn't knocked her confidence in her ability to take care of herself, *thank you very much.* She opened her mouth to tell the unseen stranger that she had it under control when the fine hairs on the back of her neck stood on end and a voice spoke, deeper, smoother and richer than the luxurious one hundred per cent cacao hot chocolate she'd indulged in that afternoon. It positively *oozed* dominance.

'Is everything okay here?'

The drunk man struggled to catch his breath, grunting as he winced.

'Get lost, jerk, I saw her first.'

She could practically *feel* the disdain radiating from the newcomer and unexpectedly something kicked low in her gut.

'Everything is just fine,' Elle countered lightly, determined not to reveal quite how her heart was hammering in her chest, though whether it was adrenalin from the confrontation or the unexpected impact of her would-be rescuer, she couldn't be sure.

'I have the situation under control,' she added quietly.

The dark shadow appeared in her peripheral vision and a decidedly muscular figure moved to insert himself between her and her misguided suitor, but Elle twisted her wrist and pushed her other hand over another barely imperceptible notch so that he went from red to puce. His friend was opening and closing his mouth but not moving to help.

'Like I said,' she repeated firmly, 'it's under control. The gentlemen were just leaving for some much-needed fresh air. Isn't that right, boys?'

'Okay, okay,' he gasped. 'We're leaving.'

Similarly, her would-be hero took a half-step backwards in tacit acknowledgment that she did indeed have matters in hand, though he did remain close as if for back-up should she need it. Elle appreciated both actions, even as the drunk man stumbled backwards, nursing his hand and shooting her a baleful look before appearing to realise he was free again. His eyes gleamed and

he stood his ground, jutting his chin out pugna-
ciously. She opened her mouth to issue another
warning, but this time the stranger beat her to it.

'There isn't a problem here, is there, lads?'

It ought to have been a question but it wasn't.
The stranger's physical presence only emphasised
his strength, and yet somehow he managed to
make it do it without actually crowding the men
or looking as though he was threatening them.

Her eyes were still firmly locked on the drunken
man—something warned her that to look at the
stranger directly would be as dangerous as staring straight into the sun. Elle tried to sound dis-
approving out of the corner of her mouth.

'I really can handle him. But thanks.'

'He's drunk and humiliated. You have no idea
which way he'll jump,' the liquid gold voice murmured.

'Besides, that was one impressive thumb-lock
you executed back there. I'd fancied myself to
have been swooping in here like some modern-
day superhero when I saw you almost fall off your
stool before. At least throw me this bone now so
I don't feel completely impotent.'

There was something utterly secure in the
stranger's tone that made Elle smile. She doubted

this man had ever felt anything close to impotent
in his whole life. In any sense of the word. And
his compliment had warmed her far more than it
perhaps ought to have.

'Then far be it from me to emasculate you.' She
covered her mouth with her hand to hide her sudden, irrepressibly inane grin.

Then, crossing her leather-trouser-clad legs on
the bar stool—the brand-new purchase intended
to lift her spirits—she gestured discreetly.

'Be my guest.'

Without another word the stranger stepped forward. Goose-bumps coursed along Elle's arms
and over her skin and for one long second her
gaze lingered on a tight backside and muscular
thighs, all wrapped up in black jeans, then slowly
travelled upwards. He was tall, very tall, and sol-
idly built, with a black T-shirt seemingly following every contour of his exquisitely hewn torso.

She blinked—*since when did she ogle?*—before
forcing herself to focus on what he was saying.

'Well, lads? Didn't you say you were leaving?'
he said, offering the men a way of backing down
while still allowing them the appearance of keeping their dignity.

It was a pretty impressive skill, which was sadly

lost on the drunken duo. One of them craned his head up to glower, swaying precariously.

'D'you wanna fight, or shhomething?'

'I don't, particularly.' The response was even, conversational, but there was no mistaking the ominous tone. 'But if that's really how you'd like to end your evening…?'

For a moment everything seemed to hang. And then, to Elle's relief, the one turned to his mate, muttering something about her not being worth the effort, and slunk away into the crowd. Still, the stranger watched with his arms folded across his chest making his biceps bunch appealingly from behind, and shifted his weight from one foot to the other. Poised, controlled, but ready if they suddenly returned.

'Better?' she asked him, once she was sure the men had left.

Affecting nonchalance, she deliberately plucked a non-existent stray thread from her thigh, wondering who had removed all her internal organs and replaced them with a veritable butterfly pavilion.

'Much, thanks,' he agreed with no trace of embarrassment, pulling a comical pose as he flexed his muscles. 'I feel like a man again.'

She finally made herself look at him properly, and the instant she did she found she couldn't drag her gaze away.

And what a man.

He was strong, fit—Stevie had been fit, his football giving him an enviable physique—but this was something...*more.* A whole different level. The stranger had a dangerous power about him that seemed to emanate from the inside just as much as the view on the outside. He was commanding, impressive, *thrilling.* She'd worked with plenty of majors and colonels and brigadiers in her career, but this guy eclipsed them all.

Was this what she'd been missing all these years?

She barely resisted cocking her head to assess him more thoroughly. Lookswise, his face was inarguably masculine with a defined jawline and a blade of a nose. Not pretty-boy handsome, but far more arresting. The kind of face that would be imprinted in her mind for ever. Greedily she drank in the view. From the honed, squared jaw to the tiny crinkle lines around his eyes, which seemed to add character, it was a face that could have stopped a whole bar full of women and, if the daggers she could feel in her back even now were anything to go in, already had.

Unreadable and intense, his eyes were a smoky blue-grey and were were focussed entirely on her. They drew her in and refused to release her, and so help her she didn't want to go anywhere. Forget the butterflies; now a hundred tiny fireflies had sprung up in her belly like a magical light show on a warm summer evening.

She couldn't decide whether it was thrilling or nerve-racking. She flicked her tongue out to moisten nervous lips.

Something momentarily flared in his eyes, something that sent the fireflies racing for cover as fire spread through her entire torso and her heart pounded so hard it would surely leave black and-blue marks on the inside of her chest.

'Where did you learn to do that thumb-lock, incidentally? Very *Jane Bond*... You're not army, by any chance?'

Something about his tone made Elle hesitate, as if it was more important to him than he would have preferred to let on. Maybe he was one of those blokes who hated the military, or one who got a kick out of a woman in uniform? Either way, tonight she didn't want to be Major Caplin, Dr

Caplin, or even Gabriella Caplin. She just wanted to be Elle.

'Self-defence class when I was a uni student,' she answered, not untruthfully.

'Ah.'

She might have been imagining it, but she could have sworn he relaxed. *So, not a military fan, then.*

'Are you okay?'

'Fine,' she croaked out. 'Thanks.'

She was jerking her head like she'd just electrocuted herself.

'Are you always so effective at shooting a guy down?'

'I don't know where that came from.' She shrugged. 'He put his hand on me and I just reacted, but I had tried ignoring him first. I thought he might have gone away.'

The stranger nodded sagely.

'Ah, you see, that's where you went wrong,' he continued deadpan. 'That's a polite woman's logic. A drunken man just thinks, *She hasn't told me to sod off yet, she must be interested.*'

Elle laughed. She couldn't help it. Some of the awkwardness dissipated.

'I see. Well, thanks, I'll remember that for the next time.'

A small smiled tugged at those irrationally tempting lips of his.

'At the risk of a knee to my most valued possessions, can I buy you a drink?'

For the first time that evening, Elle was actually tempted. More than tempted. And it only had a little to do with the devilish grin he'd just flashed, which turned her insides out, and more to do with the man flashing it.

But something made her stall.

It could have been the fact that she'd been about to head for the door before the unpleasant interlude with the drunken duo. But Elle suspected it was more to do with the fact that this man here was ridiculously hot, making her brain turn to treacle and her tongue forget how to function. She'd come here to rediscover herself, not pick someone up. And if she accepted a drink from him, would he think she was somehow…obligated to more? She had no idea, but she was sure *that* wasn't going to happen. Still, what were the rules? How did she go about this flirtation dance stuff? The last time she'd dated had been fourteen years ago.

'I have a drink,' she managed, buying herself time to think.

'Which is no doubt warm and unpleasant since you've been cradling it for the last hour.'

She wasn't sure whether to be feel pleased or creeped out. Something about the guy made her feel more the former than the latter.

'You've been watching me.'

His chuckled. A rich, warm sound that made her stomach flip-flop.

'I wouldn't say *watching* exactly, that might sound a bit…off, don't you think? I happened to be getting the drinks in when we first arrived.'

We?

'You're with someone?' She tried to remind herself that she had no right to feel so disappointed.

'Over there.'

She followed the direction he indicated, the ridiculous beam rushing back to her face.

'A lads' night out?'

'I'm glad that delights you so much,' he commented wryly, turning to the bar with a minimal dip of his head to attract the bartender's attention. 'I think I'll take that as a good sign and order you a fresh drink after all.'

Elle gave herself a mental kick. She had some good qualities, she knew that. Her colleagues generally described her as focussed and driven yet also fun and bubbly, and she prided herself on her ability to master a curveball, but she never had mastered the art of flirting. She'd never had to. And right now she felt about as sophisticated as turning up to an officers' garden party wearing jeans and a white tee. Yet somehow the obvious appreciation in his gaze stopped her from feeling too gauche.

She was still trying to work out her next move a few moments later as the bartender carefully removed her tepid half-consumed drink and re-placed it with a fresh one.

'How did you do that?' she marvelled, with a glance at the frantically waved notes in the crowd as customers still clamoured for attention. 'It was like magic.'

'No magic, we've just got a tab going. And we tip well.'

'You come here often?'

Oh, Lord, had she really said that?

'Not really, but when we do it's usually an all-out affair.' He grinned, and white-hot attraction seared through her, turning her inside out. Elle swallowed hard, forcing herself to remain non-chalant.

'Celebration?'

'Call it a bit of a…leaving do.'

Moments later a generous glass of dark liquid was set quietly in front of the stranger. Elle glanced at the fizzing bubbles in surprise.

'You're on soft drinks?'

'I don't drink.' He shrugged casually.

'Ah.'

Recovering alcoholic? That explained a lot. Like why a guy who looked like he did was still single. And that unexpected bitterness to his earlier comment about not knowing how the drunken guy was going to react.

'Maybe the odd glass of wine if I'm dining out, but I'm generally happy to be the designated driver on a night out like this,' he added, as if he'd read her mind. 'Easier than trying to get a taxi sometimes.'

Yet she didn't miss the flash of…something that skittered across his face before he shot it down.

So he wasn't the drunk, but maybe someone close to him?

She gave herself a mental shake at her uncharacteristic curiosity.

What did it matter? It wasn't any of her business.

Admittedly, she'd dealt with enough soldiers

telling her only half-truths about their injuries in order to get back to their unit quicker. If you knew the give-aways it could be easy to spot when someone was holding back, even if you had no idea *what* they were withholding. But this wasn't the army now. She wasn't at work. This was about play. So if this stranger wanted to keep something private then who was she to pry?

She smiled openly.

'So, you aren't going back to them? Your friends?'

'Do you want me to?'

She should tell him it didn't matter to her either way. Hadn't she been ready to leave anyway for the comforts of her hotel spa bath and downy bed? Instead, she held out her hand by way of silent invitation.

'I'm Elle.'

'*Just* Elle?' He smiled, stretching out his arm.

His fingers brushed hers moments before a strong palm enveloped her hand. Something arced between them, making the air seem to crackle. It was all Elle could do not to snatch her hand back.

Or to lean into him and give in to the rash impulse to press her mouth to those inviting lips.

'Well, then, Just Elle, I'm just Fitz.'

'Touché.'

She couldn't help a soft chuckle from slipping out and the instant flare of awareness from the stranger—from Fitz—instilled her with another unexpected boost of confidence.

The guy who was coveted by a good proportion of the females in the place actually fancied her? From something as simple as her laugh?

'So, Elle, what brings you here tonight? Alone? Only—and forgive me if this sounds impertinent—aside from your impressive moves back there with your unwanted admirers, you've looked a little...uncomfortable all evening.'

She offered a rueful smile.

'Was it that obvious?'

'You mean aside from the ramrod-straight back? Or the untouched drink? Or the fact that most people are happy to flirt yet you were oblivious to the five or six other, non-inebriated men who tried to make a play for you all evening?'

'Are you saying I don't fit in?' She couldn't help teasing him, firmly quashing the slither of unease that he might have a point.

'I'm saying you looked a little like you weren't used to it.'

She sighed. She could try to be nonchalant, but

it wasn't likely to work. Maybe she should just be honest? She had opened her mouth to speak when a commotion on the other side of the room caught her attention. But as the people jostled she caught sight of a body on the floor, convulsing as a screaming girl tried to hold it down.

Elle didn't think, she didn't wait, she just glanced at her watch to note the time and she acted.

CHAPTER TWO

ONE MOMENT ELLE was sitting on the barstool next to him, the next she was thrusting people out of her way as she made a beeline for some hubbub behind him. Call it intuition after fifteen years as an army officer, call it something about Elle's understated purposefulness, but Fitz was compelled to follow even as he strained to see past the throng.

It was only when he saw the young man on the floor, with Elle gently forcing a sobbing girl to release her grip on him, that Fitz realised what was happening. Icy fingers slid the length of his spine, the length of his body, rooting him to the spot. He fought to shut his mind to the memories that threatened to overtake him, but not fast enough. They slammed into him with brutal force, knocking his breath out like a bullet striking body armour.

The last time he'd seen someone having a seizure like this had been over twenty years ago. His baby sister had had seizures from about the age of one. Not often, but still. *How had he forgotten about that?*

Memories crowded his head. Images he'd buried along with her body. Her tiny, five-year-old's coffin next to the adult-size one of their mother. He struggled to shove the unwanted images away and try instead to focus on helping the woman he'd just met who was managing the situation with the same cool efficiency with which she'd dispatched Tweedle-Dum and Tweedle-Dumber earlier.

'Let him go,' Elle was telling the girl, kindly but firmly.

'No. No. I can't.' She shook her head manically and tried to shrug Elle off. 'He's my brother, he's going to hurt himself.'

'How long has your brother suffered from epilepsy?'

'What? No.' The girl shook her head violently. 'He's seventeen, he doesn't have epilepsy. He's *never* had epilepsy. What's wrong with him?'

'Your brother's never had a seizure before?' Elle asked calmly.

The same calmness with which Fitz remembered his mother teaching his eleven-year-old self what to do if his sister ever had a seizure if he was alone with her. Not that he'd ever needed to in the end.

'Of course he's never had one,' the girl was wailing. 'I told you, there's nothing wrong with him.'

'What about anyone else in your family?'

'What? No. I'm his sister, I'd *know* if he had epilepsy.' The girl was practically apoplectic. 'I have to make sure he doesn't hurt himself. Oh, God, what's wrong with him?'

'It's okay.' Taking the girl's head in her hands, Elle forced the kid to look at her. 'I'm a doctor, do you understand me? It's going to be okay but you have to trust me. Let go of your brother. If you try to hold him in place you could end up causing more damage.'

Her soothing tone not only seemed to help the girl but him too, and he began to be able to move past his memories just as she glanced up at the room, her stern, clear voice carrying over the now music-free club.

'Everyone else, can you just back up, please, and give him some room?' She turned back to the girl. 'Okay, now this is what you're going to do. You're going to move that table away for me so your brother doesn't hurt himself by banging it.'

All of a sudden Fitz's legs sprang back into life and, propelling himself forward, he distracted the girl.

'Come on, I'll help you. We need to move everything else out of the way. You move those bottles and glasses onto the table down there and I'll move the table itself, understand? Great, okay, now we should move those chairs and the stool.'

His mind and body acting in slick, smooth unison, the way he'd honed them to ever since he'd joined the army, Fitz eased himself even further away from the unwelcome, debilitating memories. Instead, he concentrated on Elle and trying to preempt her needs, passing her a jumper, which she took with a silent nod, balled up and slid under the boy's head to cushion it. Then he placed himself between the peering crowd and the boy.

'That's all, folks,' he said authoritatively. 'If you don't need to be here, I suggest you move away and get back to your own affairs. There's nothing to see here.'

He nodded with satisfaction as the crowd immediately began to dissipate, but he was hardly surprised when there were a few reluctant to leave, one of whom was even reaching for his mobile phone.

'*Now*,' Fitz growled, taking a step closer so that he was invading the guy's personal space without making actual physical contact.

It felt as though ever since he'd seen Elle his night had been one incident after another when usually a night out for him, in the rare downtime he had as a colonel, was fairly uneventful.

What was it about this woman, the emerald-eyed redhead, that seemed to turn his world up-side down? She was so damned captivating. But as much as he was loath to admit it, he suspected it wasn't simply about her striking looks, even if they were what had drawn him from almost the first minute his group had walked into the club.

So she was a doctor?

He didn't like to examine quite how relieved that made him feel. Something about her attitude and confidence had seemed so familiar, he'd suspected she might be military. It wouldn't be surprising. They were close to a mobilisation army barracks, which was how his group of fellow officers knew about the club. It was one they always frequented before they went on a tour of duty. The place was more bar than pub, and, though it had a dance-floor, it was not a nightclub, so as officers they could be comfortable having a night out without risking running into the junior ranks, who typically opted for the pubs and bars in the centre of town, which would be heaving with soldiers over the next few nights.

But the idea of Elle potentially being military had been more of a let-down than it perhaps should have been. That would have been the one obstacle to make him walk away. Not that there was any military reason that would prevent them from getting together, of course—as a doctor she would be a commissioned officer just as he was—but, still, it was a line he had always refused to cross for his own personal reasons. Ever since Janine. But Fitz suspected Elle might have made him consider breaking his unnecessarily strict personal rules.

He wasn't yet prepared to examine why he had been so pleased that the fact that she was a doctor, and not military, meant he didn't have to find out.

'Fitz?' Elle's voice broke into his reverie. 'Can you call for an ambulance? Tell them a seventeen-year-old male is suffering from a seizure with no known history of epilepsy.'

Without waiting for his response, as though trusting him implicitly, she lowered her head to check on the boy then turned back to the girl with a gentle smile.

'What's your name?'

'Lisa.' The girl sniffed.

'Okay, Lisa, can you contact your parents?'

'Our parents? Oh, God, I can't call them, they'll kill us. They'll kill *me*. Adam's only seventeen.'

'Has your brother consumed alcohol?' Fitz heard Elle ask as he slid his mobile from his back pocket. 'Don't worry, I don't care how old you are, I just need you to tell me the truth so that I can look after him the best way I can.'

'Yes,' Lisa sobbed.

'Okay, that's fine. Do you know how much?'

'A lot. We both had a lot. Oh, this is all my fault, isn't it?'

Fitz stepped away as the emergency services operator came on the line, and gave their location and the details. After a brief check of the boy he made his way over to the bar and asked for a blanket and then made sure the crowd had dissipated. By the time he turned back to Elle, Lisa was just about calming down as her brother was slowly coming around.

'My parents are going to *kill* me.'

'Shh, you're okay, Adam,' Elle soothed, checking her watch again. 'You just had a little seizure, but you're safe and your sister's here.'

'The ambulance is on its way,' Fitz muttered quietly. 'This is for his bladder. I'm going out to check the car, I've probably got spare clothes in my gym bag in the boot.'

Gratefully, Elle took the blanket and laid it over the boy's lap, asking him how he felt and trying to note his clarity of answers through Lisa's panicked interference. It was clearly going to be a lot easier for Elle to make her assessment without Adam's sister wailing and babbling.

'Come with me, Lisa,' Fitz commanded softly, in the tone he used when he needed people to do things he knew they absolutely didn't want to do. 'We'll work it out, but your parents need to know. However mad you think they're going to be, imagine how upset and angry they would feel if you didn't contact them.'

Almost against her will, Lisa backed away from her brother, her eyes still locked on his dazed form.

'I... I guess they'd be even more angry?'

'I think you're probably right. Now, my...friend is going to stay with Adam until the ambulance arrives, but you and I need to call your parents together and let them know what's going on.'

'And tell them Adam's going to need to go to hospital for an EEG,' Elle muttered in a low voice. 'Tell them to meet Lisa and Adam there.'

'Understood.' He turned back to the sister. 'Right, shall we step outside where it's a little quieter?'

The sister flip-flopped again.

'No, no... I *can't*.'

Time to take her properly in hand.

'Lisa, they're going to find out some time,' Fitz informed her sternly. 'Better sooner, don't you think? If you'd prefer, I can call them for you, but someone needs to do it. Now.'

The girl hesitated, then nodded, silently handed over her mobile, and followed him outside.

'Thanks for moving everyone away so quickly,' Elle said forty minutes later as they watched the ambulance pull away from the kerb. 'The last thing that kid needed was to come round to find a bar full of nosy people gawking at him.'

'No problem. You were quite impressive back there. Again.' He smiled. 'Shall we go back inside?'

She shook her head.

'No, I really *do* need to go. But thanks for the drink.'

Her guarded gaze caught him by surprise. He couldn't shake the feeling he was missing something. The sounds of the music thumped sensually into the street from the live band who had taken the stage early to lift the mood of the still stunned crowd, but neither of them made a move.

'Ah, okay. I did find one thing odd, though,' Fitz said, stalling for time. 'His sister really had no idea he was epileptic?'

'He might not be.' Elle cocked her head, apparently happy to be delayed. 'It isn't uncommon to have a single seizure and then for it never to happen again for the rest of his life. Especially because he's seventeen and alcohol can be a trigger. The EEG should help to determine whether or not there is unusual electrical activity in Adam's brain and he'll go from there.'

'And what do you think?' Fitz asked, admiring the way her eyes lit up when she talked about medicine. Clearly being a doctor was more than just a job to her, it was something she loved.

'I don't know without the results, but from everything he said afterwards, I'm thinking he's had a few absence seizures in the past, which he never really thought much about. Then the combination of alcohol, exams in school, finding it hard to sleep at night was a trigger for more. But that's just a guess.' She hunched her shoulders. 'Anyway, from your reactions I'm guessing that isn't the first time you've seen a seizure either?'

'My little sister suffered from epilepsy. From the first year of her life.'

The words were out before Fitz had time to think and he halted abruptly. He never talked about his sister. *Never.*

The last time he'd even talked about his family—other than to trot out the one, practised sentence that his mother and sister had died a long time ago—had been to Janine. And even then he hadn't told her the full story, just enough to satisfy her questions after her colonel father had already told her about the car crash.

He'd certainly never told her about those three years when it had just been his mother, his sister and himself in that tiny, cramped flat. The happiest three years of their lives together until his old man had walked back in that night.

'Suffered? Past tense?' Elle asked. 'Did she grow out of it? I think it's somewhere around ninety percent of children with childhood absence epilepsy can grow out of it by about the age of twelve, although I understand they can sometimes have other types of seizure.'

'No. She died.'

Elle held his gaze steadily, her expression changing.

'I'm so sorry. What happened?'

Old, familiar guilt had resurrected itself, and was pressing on his chest like a flatbed truck was crushing him. Images assailed Fitz. Him getting home, the car gone, the phone lying smashed on the floor, the shattered furniture, leaving the house turned upside down. And everywhere the stench of booze. The stench of *him*. The man who was Fitz's father in name only.

'Car crash. She was six, nearly seven. My mother died too.'

He braced himself for the *look*, pity coupled with discomfort as they quickly changed the topic. Instead, he simply saw quiet empathy, a calmness and genuine interest. It seemed to slice through all the layers of protective armour he'd spent years pulling into place.

'Fitz, how awful for you. So it was just you and your father?'

'He was driving.' Fitz tried to swallow the words. Elle was a stranger and this was no one's business except his. 'Drunk. I was the only one left.'

Instead, they kept pouring out, as if they'd been waiting for this moment—for this woman—for half his lifetime.

'Is that why you wanted to protect me from the drunken bloke who was hassling me at the bar, and his mate?' she asked softly. 'So, how old were you?'

'Sorry?' he stalled.

This was the longest he'd allowed himself to think about it in a long, long time. And he didn't want to. Not here. Not now. Not ever.

'How old were you when your family died?' she repeated steadily.

'You ask a lot of questions for a damsel in distress.'

'I wasn't in distress. I had my thumb-lock, remember?' Another smile that twisted in his gut. 'But that's not to say I didn't appreciate the solid back-up.'

'Well, then, that makes me feel better.' He managed a wry smile.

He should have known better than to distract

her. Her gaze never wavered and he was compelled to address her unanswered question.

'Seventeen. But it was the night of my eighteenth.'

He should have had happy memories of the time but all he had was one of his mother and his sister lying in that hospital mortuary. To this day he didn't know which of the mass of bruises over his mother's face had been caused by the crash itself and which had been the result of his drunkard father's cruel fists. Fitz struggled to breathe, let alone regulate his voice, which sounded a million miles away when he spoke.

'Listen, this isn't something I like to talk about.'

A beat passed before Elle answered, but not before reaching out to run a hand over his cheek as if she actually cared. And the oddest thing was, he felt like she did.

'Maybe you *should* talk.'

'I don't need to talk,' he bit out.

She gave an apologetic shrug, but it didn't stop her from continuing.

'I'm sorry. I know it's probably none of my business but I'm a doctor. I can see the signs when someone has repressed things for a long time. Es-

pecially soldiers who think they're too tough to
need to talk and repress all kinds of bad incidents.'

'What makes you think I'm a soldier?' he asked
sharply.

'Those spare gym trousers you gave to the boy
in there after his seizure had made him lose bladder control? I couldn't help noticing they were
military issue. And there's just something about
the way you handle yourself. I'm guessing Infantry?'

The way she smiled, polite but with none of the
openness or interest of earlier, made him sure that
discovering he was military had put her off. Ironically, his experience with women was that it was
usually the other way around.

'Not Infantry but, yes, I'm army. A colonel,' he
confirmed, technically not a full colonel, a lieutenant colonel, but he doubted that would make a
difference to her.

Neither would the fact that until a couple of
months ago he'd been a major in a different Royal
Engineers regiment. Now he was at the start of
his two-year posting as commanding officer of
his very own regiment.

Yet right now all he could think was that something about the army meant that Elle was about

to walk away from him, and a part of him desperately wanted her to stay. He wondered if she had a brother, a father who had served and been hurt. Or worse.

'You don't like it that I'm in the army, do you?'

'No, no. It isn't that. It's…complicated.'

'Too complicated to finish that drink with me?'

She sucked in a deep breath, as though trying to make her mind up about something. It was unsettling how much he wanted to spend more time with her. A drink, an hour, maybe the rest of the evening, whatever she was prepared to offer. He couldn't recall the last time he'd ever wanted to spend time with any woman like this. But at least now her determination to leave had faded and she was looking decidedly undecided.

'After the last hour, I'm guessing both of us would benefit from a bit of fun now,' he pressed. 'A bit of a laugh? A drink? Maybe a dance?'

'I don't dance.' She frowned uncertainly but didn't refuse him.

She was torn. He still didn't know exactly what had put her off before but she was clearly as attracted to him as he was to her.

It didn't make sense. He'd had short-term relationships and a handful of one-night stands over the years, all with attractive women of varying intelligence, but there was something different about Elle that seemed to pull at his gut and not just at the other, more...*obvious* part of his anatomy. Something glowed, like a whisper of wind over dying embers, inside Fitz; somewhere that had been a gnawing void for longer than he could remember.

He snorted silently inside his head. It was physical attraction, pure and simple. It was just the unusual circumstances of their meeting that had given rise to such a fanciful notion. The unexpected memory of his baby sister and the life he'd long since forgotten.

He hadn't really wanted to come out tonight, the eighteenth anniversary of his mother and sister's deaths. Its echoes of celebration seemed cruelly hollow. From today, his life had been devoid of their love and laugher and warmth for longer than they had been a part of it. Hardly a night for letting loose.

But he didn't have a choice. It was a long-standing tradition with the men with whom he'd gone through Royal Military Training Academy—officer cadets over a decade earlier—to come on a final night out before a tour of duty. To have reneged on it would have raised questions Fitz didn't want to answer.

And so he'd come, and from the minute he'd walked in and headed to the bar to buy the first round, his gaze had snagged on the arresting woman with the stunning red hair. A glorious, waist-length curtain of vibrant golds and reds and coppers that had evoked long-buried memories of the vivid autumn day over a decade earlier when he'd returned, exhilarated and hooked after his first ever tour of duty. It had tugged at something primal, deep inside him, yet…something he still couldn't quite identify had also held him back from approaching her immediately.

Then those drunken idiots had given him the excuse he'd pretended he hadn't been looking for, only to find that she could take care of herself with aplomb, and he'd been even more intrigued.

Fitz reminded himself that tonight was about fun, having a good time. In a matter of days he'd be thousands of miles away in a geographically hostile—though for once non-combat—environment and neck-deep in responsibility for his engineers' role in a crucial, multi-discipline, hearts-and-minds mission. Tonight was his last chance to blow off some steam.

'I don't believe you can't dance.' He grinned. 'But if that's true, how about I teach you?'

'You dance?'

Her brows knitted together and his stomach pulled tight. *Man, she was cute.* He shoved his hands into his trousers to counter the sudden impulse to take her face in his hands and kiss the frown lines away.

'Not like some of those guys in there who can set the floor on fire.' He lifted his shoulders. 'But I can move my feet and keep a decent beat. So what do you say?'

CHAPTER THREE

FITZ COULD MORE than just hold a decent beat, Elle thought an hour or so later as they took a break from another round of dancing in order to get a much-needed drink. He wasn't competition standard, but he had a few nice moves and she was enjoying herself far more than she could have dreamed a couple of hours ago. She was glad she hadn't left.

She'd been going to when she'd realised he was army. Not that she had to, it wasn't against the rules given their ranks, but it was a complication she wasn't sure she needed. And then he'd told her about his family and she'd felt a connection to him. The patent physical attraction between them only partially explained the draw; he'd trusted her enough to tell her, and that made it easier for her to feel she could trust him too.

Especially after Stevie.

'Water, please.' She nodded gratefully as he asked her what she wanted, trying not to read too much into the fact that his hand was still curled gently around her smaller one. 'Or an orange juice. I could really go for an ice-cold juice right about now. Wait, I'll come with you.'

'Fine,' Fitz agreed. 'Just stay close.'

Her heart hammered even harder than it had been doing all evening as he pulled her casually to him and began to lead her through the throng to the bar. Then, reaching for a free sample of a lurid-coloured shot, he sniffed it warily.

'You sure you just want water? You could try this Diablo's Poison they've been pushing all night. I mean, it looks like some hacked jet engine fuel, smells even worse, and would probably strip your insides for the year, but if you can down it in one go you get a selfie and a photo on their media site. I mean, what's not to love?'

He faked choking and Elle laughed, a rich feeling that seemed to bubble up out of nowhere, washing away the very last vestiges of the grime and sadness of the last few weeks. She was beginning to feel more and more like her old self with every passing moment. Stevie hadn't got the better of her, and she wasn't making quite the fool out of herself with this flirting business, as she'd initially feared. His betrayal had knocked her back but it hadn't devastated her.

If anything, tonight's unexpected turn of events had reminded her that Stevie had nothing to do with all the best qualities she prided herself on having: her skill as a doctor; her ability to take care of herself; her appeal to someone like Fitz. She didn't know what it was about Fitz that seemed to lift her the way he did, she just knew the more time she was in his company the more time she wanted to spend with him.

And the fact that he'd confided in her earlier—things about his family that he didn't tell many people, if any—had allowed her to let her guard down with him. As though she knew him, rather than had just met him. Another side to the man she could easily see as a strong colonel, a dynamic leader, an inspiring mentor.

'You look more relaxed than you were earlier,' Fitz said suddenly, ordering the drinks and then turning to her.

His gaze was unexpectedly more penetrating than before, reminding her that her body was tantalisingly close to his.

Abruptly, she ached for more.

They'd been dancing for over an hour, yet it had

been so fast-paced that this was probably the closest she'd been to him for any length of time. And her body seemed acutely aware of it.

'I *feel* more relaxed,' Elle admitted, ignoring the irony as she struggled to regulate her breathing, and control the goose-bumps of anticipation from racing over her skin.

'So, what brought you here tonight?'

She drew in a sharp breath.

'Why ask that now, particularly?' she managed slowly.

His mouth curved up into the seductive smile that she'd already discovered turned her insides out.

'Because, I'd very much like to kiss you.' He didn't let her break the gaze for a moment. Direct and concise, just what she'd come to expect from Fitz. 'But I don't think that's what you were looking for when you first came in here.'

'Astute of you,' Elle murmured, trying to buy herself some time.

It was as though the evening had been leading up to this point from the moment he'd stepped up to her at the bar. Now it was up to her to decide whether dancing, a drink, a laugh were as far as things went, or if she wanted more with Fitz to-night.

He didn't answer. He didn't rush her. He simply waited. And Elle was mesmerised by the way his thumb traced lazy, circular patterns over the back of her hand, as though the two of them had all the time in the world.

With his other hand, he reached between their bodies and picked up her drink from the bar to offer it to her before taking his own.

'Come on,' he muttered, turning and leading her back through the mass of rhythmically throbbing bodies and to a quieter corner of the club.

Then he turned back to face her, his gaze snagging hers as easily as before.

Dragging her eyes away, she took a fortifying gulp of orange juice.

Then a second.

Finally, she lifted her gaze back to Fitz.

'I was in a relationship. Two weeks ago I discovered he'd been cheating on me. I admit that it knocked me. I walked out and have been staying in the hotel up the road ever since. I suppose you might say I've been licking my wounds.'

She offered a rueful smile but Fitz just frowned.

'Long-term relationship?'

'Fourteen years,' she confirmed.

He let out a low whistle.

'That must be tough. You were serious about this guy, then?'

He tailed off and Elle could guess what he was probably thinking.

'Only I don't seem as cut up about it as you'd have thought?'

'I'm not judging.'

She shrugged.

'I was hurt, humiliated. I felt betrayed. I sat in that hotel room and felt like a prize idiot. I felt as though I didn't know who I was.' She'd wondered if she was less of a woman, less sexy, less desirable. Not that she was about to tell Fitz that. 'And then I had what I call my "light-bulb" moment; I realised it was more about my pride being hurt than me actually *being* hurt, and I asked myself why I was letting someone else's actions shake my belief in myself.'

'That's very logical.' Fitz didn't look convinced. 'Very controlled.'

She smiled wistfully.

'Isn't that the point? I realised we'd been growing apart for a very long time. He was a…sportsman.' No need to name names. 'He spent a lot of time training and travelling. And my career is very demanding. I think a part of me was still in love with the idea of childhood sweethearts, when in reality we'd fallen out of love a long time ago. We didn't see each other like regular couples tend to, and we weren't really bothered.'

If she calculated it—which she hadn't been able to stop herself from doing a couple of times over the last fortnight—between multiple tours of duty, training courses and postings around the country, she doubted she'd spent more than thirty long weekends and a handful of week-long or fortnight R&Rs in Stevie's company over the last decade or so. At best a couple of hundred days.

'We didn't even live together. We always had our own homes, blaming it on the distance, but that was just an excuse. As the money rolled in, each apartment became more and more blingy, and they weren't my style. I visited but he never gave me my own key. I never needed one, but I guess I now know why he was afraid I might just pop in unannounced.'

'So that was how you found out? You decided to surprise him with a visit?'

'The doorman recognised me and let me in, sweet old guy who only did a couple of nights to top up his pension. I don't know whether he knew the girls were up there, or if he did but thought it was time I knew what Stevie was up to. First time I'd surprise visited in years. Pretty dumb, huh?'

'Only if you're talking about him.' Fitz's thunderous expression somehow soothed her bruised ego.

Elle wrinkled her nose.

'It wasn't just Stevie's fault. I liked my own space, too. I think in the last ten years we might have seen each other two hundred days. Two hundred days out of three thousand, six hundred and fifty-two-ish.'

Her stomach rolled with guilt.

She'd been pretty much fine with that—they both had, by the end—but in the very beginning how many keys had Stevie offered her? In the beginning how many times had he begged her to visit more? To come to his major league matches? To attend some B-list party? And she'd always found an army-related excuse not to. Then again, where had Stevie been when she'd finally graduated or passed out of her Sandhurst course? Out with his teammates, celebrating his own big wins. Too busy to come to either of the two biggest days in her life.

So what did that tell her about the state of their relationship? They'd had three years as teenagers in the flush of first love unable to stand being apart for even a maths lesson, to adults who hadn't blinked an eye at being apart for three months at a time. Or, at least, *she* hadn't. But, still, she would never have dreamed of cheating on him and it wasn't as though she hadn't had the opportunity over the years.

Yet Stevie had. A wave of sadness washed over her. He hadn't always been that way. He'd changed. Fame had changed him. And, as if to add clichéd insult to even more clichéd injury, his excuse had been that the two bimbos 'meant nothing', that they were 'football groupies', that as a professional footballer he was a 'high-profile target' who had done well to resist their seduction skills as often as he had.

She'd taken time to get her head around *that* prize gem this last fortnight and finally seen it for the bull it was. Finally, he had professed that he couldn't be blamed for being lonely and needing physical comfort given how often her work kept her away from him. And *that* particular knife of guilt had been the one to actually lodge in her back.

She shook her head and took another long drink.

'So why stay in a hotel?' he asked curiously. 'Why not just go back to your own home?'

'I didn't want him to follow me down here. I didn't want him to find me.'

She didn't want to do something stupid like let him cry and beg and guilt her into taking him back.

'Anyway, it's not a subject I want to dwell on. I came here to prove to myself that I could enjoy a night out in my own company. I didn't bank on how eventful it would be, but I've felt more like myself than ever. And I guess meeting you wasn't a bad bonus.'

She managed a deliberately cheeky smile, something tightening in her chest when Fitz finally stopped frowning and laughed with her.

'Okay.' He dipped his head. 'Then what would you like to do now? Another drink? Another dance? I could just walk you back to your hotel if you've had enough.'

There was no hint of suggestion in his tone, not that Elle was expecting there to be any. Fitz was the kind of guy who didn't crowd a girl, and she appreciated it. His interest in her was clear yet at no time this evening had he made her feel under any obligation. He was utterly secure in his own skin in everything he seemed to do, and it was an incredibly attractive quality.

The funny thing was that the more he gave her space, the closer to him she wanted to get.

'I think this is what I'd like to do now.'

Before she could second-guess herself, she stretched up onto her toes and pressed her lips against his.

Vaguely she considered it might have been better if she'd remembered to set her glass down first, but then a crackle of energy shot between them and Elle forgot everything else.

Everything stopped in that instant as he bent his head. Fitz didn't merely kiss her back, he *claimed* her, expertly and devastatingly, licking through her body and firing up senses she'd never even known existed. His hands lifted to cup her head, fingers entangling their way into her hair as though he'd been waiting to touch it—to touch *her*—all evening, and Elle held herself closer to his powerful frame.

His mouth was crushing hers, tasting her, exulting in her and, in its ruthlessly exquisite way, crushing any last doubts that she somehow wasn't enough as a woman. He made her feel beautiful, and desirable, and sexy. Fitz made her feel bolder than she'd ever felt before—at least, outside her work persona—as he helped her to discover a side of herself she'd never dreamed existed. A side of herself that was revelling in every stroke of his sensual tongue.

Her fingers bit into his shoulders and she exulted in the power there. Her entire body rocked against his, almost involuntarily, in a rhythm totally apart from the music's. A rhythm as old as time, yet one that she hadn't felt for a long time. And certainly never, *ever* anything quite like this. She pulsed everywhere. Her head was in a mad spin and her chest felt like a band was being wound tightly around her. Yet however close she pressed her body against his strong, unmistakeably hard frame, it didn't feel enough. She couldn't get close enough.

His kisses were like a heavenly sin. His arms around her, locking her in place, were like a sumptuous jail. She could feel every perfect, chiselled inch of him along every inch of *her*. But it wasn't enough. She wanted more.

Apprehension slithered down her spine, rapidly overtaken by excitement.

She'd never had a one-night stand in her life.

And somehow she knew she'd never want one again. No one had ever got under her skin quite the way Fitz had, even in these few hours. And it wasn't just that she'd always been in a relationship in the past while now she was single. That alone didn't explain it. She'd worked with enough male army officers in her career to have seen plenty of impressive examples of a man, in confidence, in charisma, in looks. But even if she'd been single, none of them would have affected her quite the way Fitz did. None of them could have tempted her to do something as completely crazy and impulsive as invite them back to her hotel room.

How did she even begin to go about suggesting it?

'Can we get out of here?' She reluctantly tore her mouth from his, murmuring nervously. She licked her lips. 'Maybe go somewhere quieter?'

He peeled her body away from his and Elle was unprepared for the sudden sense of loss.

One hand on her shoulder, the other on her waist, Fitz held her away and searched her face, reading her unspoken suggestion.

'You're sure that's what you want?'

She opened her mouth to confirm it, then paused. She still hadn't told him they were both army, and she didn't want to. Tonight wasn't a night for talking *Green*, or comparing tours or barracks.

She tried to debate whether she ought to tell him or not.

Military-wise, there nothing compelling her to tell him. They were both single, both commissioned officers, and he wasn't even in the same corps as her, let alone unit, so there was no conflict. He'd mentioned he was heading out on a tour of duty, that was true, but her tour of duty was a non-combat one so Fitz could be going to a different country, not just region, from her. And even if he *was* going to the same area, that would mean he'd probably be based out of Camp Razorwire, where she'd spent the first three months of her tour.

But when she returned she would be working in the local civilian hospital almost a couple of hundred miles and about an hour's helicopter ride away. She'd be working with a different field hospital team on the first wave of a twelve-month hearts-and-minds mission to rebuild the damaged hospital and train the local doctors to carry out surgical techniques for the benefit of the population there.

There was no conflict, no issue, no need to tell him. Tonight she really *could* be Just Elle. With a clear conscience.

'Yes, I'm sure that's what I want.' She nodded.

Fitz didn't answer, he didn't move. He just perused her face again, as if making his own mind up about something.

A horrid thought occurred to her.

'Is that what you want?' she asked abruptly.

'Yes, I want you.' He didn't even hesitate. 'God, I want you.'

His simple, direct, sure response fanned that fire that seemed to burn inside her, making her feel almost feverish. The pulsing in her body redirected itself to between her legs.

'I just want to know what that hesitation was. I need to be sure.'

'That wasn't about *this*. But I guess I'll just have to convince you.'

She was proud of herself for keeping the shake out of her tone as she stepped back into his circle of space and ran her finger lightly down his sharp jawline. Then, with a whisper-light touch, she brushed her lips on his. His response was immediate, as she'd hoped it would be.

This time his kiss was hotter, hungrier, and lethally practised. His hands moving over her body trailed sparks in their wake. Her body thrummed beneath his touch and dimly she acknowledged that after sleeping with Fitz there would be no going back. She would never be the same again. *Sex* would never be the same again.

Elle trembled at the mere thought, and it seemed to spur Fitz on as he muttered against her lips.

'Then let's get out of here.'

CHAPTER FOUR

IT WAS ALL Fitz could do to keep a controlled pace, with her boots echoing quickly next to him, their arms entwined. As if he could outpace the niggle of doubt, the wondering if this was a bad idea.

Not because he didn't want her. Because he did. God knew, his body ached for her—literally. And not because he hadn't had one-night stands before. He'd had his share.

But there was something different about Elle.

It had been so subtle that he hadn't really noticed it at first. He'd been drawn in by the attraction, nothing more. The realisation had been more recent, when it was too late to do anything about it; somewhere along the line, Elle had begun to scrape away at something deep inside him. She made him feel more than just physical attraction. She piqued his interest, stirred his soul. She made him feel a connection between the two of them.

Uncovering a truth about himself that he'd buried a long time ago.

And he couldn't afford to let her.

Because the truth was that he couldn't allow himself to feel any connection. He couldn't allow himself emotions. A mutual physical attraction was one thing, but anything more and he'd end up destroying the other person.

Hadn't he learned as much from his mother? His sister? Janine?

All three of them. Crushed. Shattered. Two of them dead. All because he'd let them down, betrayed them.

Fitz had sworn he'd never let himself get close to another person to hurt them like that, and for over ten years he'd managed just that. One-night stands or short-lived relationships had kept that loneliness, that darkness at bay. His career had done the rest and Fitz didn't intend for it to end any time soon, which was easier said than done.

It was part of the natural military order that a good proportion of officers didn't progress to the next rank, with multiple majors all after a handful of lieutenant colonel postings. Fitz's aim was to become a full colonel, then brigadier beyond that. But right now there were multiple new lieutenant colonels like him, all fighting for the same single position. It was a matter of dedicating oneself to rising through the officer ranks with focus, speed and ability, sacrificing personal relationships with barely a second thought.

Now, suddenly, for the first time he found himself standing still for a moment, taking stock and wondering what his life might have been like if he'd made different choices. And he couldn't afford to think that way because there *was* no other choice for him.

He was damaged. Hadn't Janine told him so? And hadn't her father told him that he destroyed lives? Weren't his mother and sister proof of that?

'Fitz? What is it?'

It was only when Elle swung around to face him, stopping him altogether, that Fitz realised he'd slowed down to almost a standstill. He made himself look her in the eye.

It was a mistake. Emerald depths stared unblinkingly back at him, wide and intelligent.

'You understand tonight is all I can offer you?' He barely recognised the raw quality to his voice.

'I know that.'

The almost imperceptible quiver in her response gave her away. He had to force himself to continue, even as his brain was screaming at him that he was just trying to come up with excuses and he couldn't explain why.

'Yes, but do you really understand what that means?'

Elle snorted, but her eyes dropped momentarily from his as though she couldn't bring herself to look at him.

'Of course I do. I'm pretty sure the term *one-night stand* is self-explanatory.'

'And you said yourself that up until two weeks ago you'd been with one man for fourteen years. Are you sure you're prepared for a one-night stand?'

'Are you saying I'm too sweet? Because, believe me, I've heard that before.'

'There are two kinds of sweet, Just Elle: naughty and nice.' Was that really his voice, so thick and carnal? 'I'm trying to work out which one you are.'

He couldn't help himself. Lifting a finger, he traced the velvet-soft skin of her cheek. She swallowed.

'Why don't you kiss me again and find out?'

Before he realised it, he'd hooked his finger under her chin and dropped an obliging, if restrained kiss on those deliciously swollen lips.

Another mistake.

Her eyes were glassy with desire, only serving to stoke the furnace that was already consuming him from the inside out. He wanted her with a ferocity he'd never known before. Not even with Janine.

Elle might look wholesome but she tasted like pure sin, even without that wantonly lithe body pressed so tightly against his. Without knowing it, he'd already memorised everything about her, from the way that autumnal curtain tumbled and bounced past her shoulders and down her back to the way her leather trousers clung so lovingly to her feminine curves and the shimmering, metallic green top that skimmed her waist and swung to reveal a gap at the back, giving tantalisingly discreet glimpses of smooth, bare skin.

And then she stepped into him again and there was nothing discreet about the way the hard buds of her nipples pushed through the thin material, or the way his thumb seared as he slid it into the gap and ran it down her exposed back. Not to mention the seductive heat between her legs, which was pure, full-on sexy.

'What did you decide?' she managed, her breathing rapid and shallow.

That she abraded a deep, black part of himself that he couldn't allow to be exposed. That he should walk away from her now. That he wanted her with a hunger he couldn't seem to control.

'I didn't,' he growled.

'Then let me make it easier for you. Tonight I'm the naughty side of sweet, and I want you. And you said you want me too.'

The husky whisper was his undoing.

Yes, he was toxic. To forget that was to step onto a dangerous track. If he went to Elle's hotel tonight, if he slept with her—and, God, he wanted to—then that had to be it. Like any other time, like any other woman. Sex was simply sex. Whatever it was that she scraped away inside him, he could shut that down. He had to.

Fitz cupped her head in his hands and kissed her fiercely again, as if testing himself, as if proving that the physical could be split out from anything else that had no business swirling around his chest. He kissed her until his head sparked and his body ached with such intensity it was almost agony, until he was finally convinced he was back on solid ground and it was all about the physical again.

And then he grabbed her hand and led her to the hotel and into the lift, barely releasing her long enough to press the button for the floor before pulling her against him, her back up to his chest, sliding that glorious curtain of hair to one side and dipping his head on the other side to kiss the base of her neck, as she leaned back into him and sighed softly. Perfectly.

They tumbled into her room. The heavy wooden door, restrained by its soft closing mechanism, seemed to close too slowly for Elle, firing up her sense of anticipation. Then, when it finally shut with an audible click, the weight of expectation that accompanied that soft sound was unmistakeable.

For a fraction of a second she froze. She was in a bedroom, with a stranger—a hot, caring, responsible stranger, given his actions all evening, but a stranger nonetheless.

As much as she wanted to, could she really go through with this?

Instantly—impressively, too, given the evidence of his desire was pressed, hard and undeniable, against her body—Fitz pulled back from her. She was shocked at just how bereft that tiny movement made her feel.

'Last chance,' he growled. 'You can still change your mind.'

His rich, low voice thrummed with barely re-strained lust, making her pulse thready and her insides turn molten. She'd never felt so desired and so *needy*. And the fact that, even now, he was prepared to stop actually boosted her confidence that final little step.

'I don't want to change my mind,' she whispered, running her hands over the muscles that were still frustratingly covered by the material of his shirt.

'You have to be sure, Elle,' he commanded thickly. 'Because after this, I don't know how much self-control I'll have.'

A giggle escaped her lips. A result of the heady sensation that she could exert such desire in a man like Fitz. She had no doubt that, despite his words, if he had to stop at the very last second, he'd find the superhuman willpower to do so. But the idea that he could want her so urgently was a potent thought.

Carefully concealing the tremble that threatened to play havoc with her entire body, Elle slid her hand lower to cup the evidence of his need. He flexed under her touch, a rough sound rolling from deep in his throat, the combination doing strange things to her insides.

She didn't want to talk any more, she just wanted him with such an intensity it was almost frightening.

As if reading her mind, Fitz dropped his mouth to hers, his kiss every bit as demanding, skilful and dominating as it had been in the bar. It seared through her and all she could do was cling to his shoulders and let him carry her through the flames. Again and again his tongue met hers in a slow, sensual dance. Exploring, touching, tasting, breaking away frequently to take detours at an agonisingly delicious, leisurely pace, starting at one corner of her mouth, trailing along her jaw before dipping below and down her neck.

Elle shook in his arms as Fitz sprinkled short, hot kisses along her collarbone and to the sensitive hollow in the centre. He took his time, which both reassured Elle and simultaneously drove her wild. It felt as though they'd been engaging in foreplay from the moment they'd met in that bar and, if she thought about it, it was also more foreplay than she'd had in the past year in total.

It had never been like this with Stevie. Never. Not even in the beginning when everything had been new and exciting, but they'd been so inexperienced, and certainly not at the end when he'd grown accustomed to people fawning over him, too many hangers-on only too happy to please him. Both in and out of bed.

She'd never, in her wildest dreams, thought it could ever be this good. And Fitz was just getting started, but as much as this indulgent approach was setting her every nerve ending on fire, she was ready for more. *Much more.*

Then he was kissing lower. Elle wasn't quite sure how it happened, but one moment she was in his arms with both of them fully clothed, and the next they were both naked from the waist up and his skilful mouth was making its way, in a lazily winding path, down between her breasts. He cupped her in each hand, as though testing the weight of her, and then he flicked a rough thumb-pad over one nipple as his tongue played with the other. She cried out, a powerful mix of pleasure, need and relief.

It had been such a very, *very* long time since her body had been so worshipped.

Raw need throbbed between her legs and Elle actually ached to feel Fitz sliding inside her, filling her, assuaging the yawning void that had unexpectedly opened up in her soul. Vaguely she became aware of some part of her syrupy brain struggling to extricate herself, to warn her.

If it had succeeded, it might have reminded her that this was supposed to be about sex, that it had been about proving to herself that her lack of sexual experience hadn't been the problem— more like Stevie's abject failure to keep it in his pants. As it was, that logical side to her brain was drowned out while Elle was lost to the moment, lost to Fitz's touch, lost to her own body's primal reactions. She couldn't think past the hot, urgent, intoxicating sensations that were cascading through her, much less think about her ex-fiancé. She couldn't even think enough to move them to the bedroom itself; instead they stood in the vestibule, her back still against the wall to the adjoining room. To move might mean breaking contact, something she couldn't bear to do. And so Elle stayed in place, her fingers tracing that incredible physique and marvelling at the way it reacted so urgently to her touch.

Over and over he paid homage to her body, his skin slick against her, his hands expertly working their magic and stoking those internal fires until she was sure she couldn't wait any longer.

As if reading her mind, Fitz's fingers trailed over the curves of her belly, down to the waistband of her low-slung trousers, and unzipped her in one smooth action before peeling the leather down over her legs.

Glassy-eyed, Elle shucked them, along with her heels, fully expecting Fitz to stand back up to resume where he'd left off. Instead, he stayed where he was, his fingers tracking up her leg from her calf to the sensitive hollow behind her knee and then sensually caressing her inner thighs. Never rushing, always taking care, inching his way upwards with incredible control.

'Are you getting pleasure in torturing me?' Elle gasped at last.

'A little.' His devilish voice sounded thick with need and the ache between her legs intensified. 'Just as I know you're getting pleasure from me torturing you.'

'Fitz...' She barely recognised her own voice in the strangled plea.

'Hmm?'

He was doing it deliberately, she realised. Teasing her.

'Something you wanted to say, Elle?'

His fingers were there, one more caress away

from touching her where she needed him to. One inch higher. She waited, only to realise he'd stopped.

'Elle?' he prompted huskily.

He was going to make her say it.

But of course he was.

'Fitz…please…' She shifted so that his fingers should have come into contact with her.

He was too quick.

'I want you,' she managed self-consciously.

Their interaction, his teasing, it was all so much more than she was used to. And while there was no doubt that she preferred it to the mechanical routine with merely a few grunts as a soundtrack, she still wasn't quite sure what to do with this exhilarating, all-consuming side of sex.

'You want me to touch you?' he questioned wickedly.

'Fitz…'

'Like this?' Without warning he swept a finger over her.

A mere brush over the lacy fabric of her briefs, but it sent shockwaves crashing through her. She gasped, squirmed, sought him out again, but his hand was gone, sliding around to cradle her backside.

'Or like this?' he murmured.

Before she could process what he was doing, she felt his breath on her skin and then his mouth.

Hot. Urgent. Terrifying.

Elle's entire body went rigid, her eyes focussing as she pulled desperately away.

'I don't... I don't do that.'

She could barely bring herself to look at him, crouched down there, and when she did she wished she hadn't. He was frowning up at her, his eyes locking with hers, scanning, assessing, disbelieving. Like she was some kind of...freak.

'You don't *do* that?'

Elle jutted her chin out, ignoring the two bright spots of shame that seemed to be burning holes high in her cheeks.

Strangely, though, it didn't make her want to stop altogether. It didn't make her want to give up on the idea of a night together. It just made her want to get past this moment, this awkwardness, and get on with the rest of what might be to come.

'I don't do that,' she repeated, agitated. 'Can't we just...move onto something else?'

'Why don't you do that?'

Direct but firm, he clearly wasn't going to take

any excuses. But, then, Elle wasn't about to give in either.

Images of Stevie crowded her head, making her feel hemmed in. She could count on the fingers of her two hands the number of times he'd done that for her in their entire time together, and always hurried, clearly resenting it, and only ever so that she would do it in return. And his attitude had meant that she, in turn, had hated it. The feel of his hands tight on the back of her head, keeping her on him even when she wanted to move away, the way he'd groaned how good she was just to give himself the excuse that he hadn't had time to pull back at the end.

When she'd hesitantly told him she didn't like that, he'd played the guilt card, claiming that he missed her, that her career took her away too much, that she'd never have become a doctor but for him. So she'd done it, and quickly she'd decided it was too painful to go through the charade of him pretending to do the same for her. But she carried the shame of it with her, even now.

Especially now. She couldn't tell Fitz any of that. She didn't want to be that person tonight. She wanted to be the *new* Elle, the version of herself that she'd decided should be born the moment she'd finally had the courage to walk out of the only relationship with a man she'd ever known. And she wanted to keep this perfect image of Fitz. The way he touched her body and set off fireworks inside her very core, not the way he would change once he gave her cursory attention and then expected her to service him in return.

'I don't like it,' she offered at last, when his piercing gaze refused to let her off. She licked her lips uncomfortably. 'Can't we just go back to where we were before?'

'You don't *like* it?' he said, his scepticism clear.

Elle sighed. She couldn't hoodwink him, he'd never fall for it. She'd have to offer him something more. Enough truth that he would believe her, not so much that she humiliated herself.

She sucked in a deep breath.

'In the past I didn't like it. It…it wasn't very good.'

'Ah…' he murmured, the hard stare instantly softening into something else.

For a fraction of a second, Elle relaxed.

'But you will enjoy it with me,' Fitz declared. 'I can promise you that.'

Before she could move again he hooked her leg over his shoulder and pulled the scrappy fabric to one side, then, locking her in place with his hands on her backside, Fitz simply licked a path to her undoing. Pure, molten heat coursed to Elle's core. With every practised stroke of his tongue, bubbles of fire exploded in her. Still, his rhythm kept on as though he knew exactly what she needed. As though he enjoyed giving it to her. As though he enjoyed *her*.

There was no earthly way she could bring herself to move away again and though a faint voice warned her that she would pay for it sooner than she would like, Elle finally let go of her fears and gave herself up to Fitz's unhurried but unrelenting pace. Expertly bringing her to the brink once. Twice. Then the third time, when she was so wound up with pent-up need, he finally slid his finger deep inside her, his mouth sucking on the very centre of her ache.

Elle fragmented. Her fingers sliding through his hair, her hips bucking of their own accord, she lost herself and cried his name. And still Fitz didn't stop, driving her on again and again, sending another explosion rolling through her entire body. Finally, when she couldn't take any more, he eased back and stood up again, his gentle caresses assuring her that they weren't done yet.

By the time Elle finally started to come down from the incredible high he'd just gifted her, reality had started to kick in. He was going to expect her to return the favour. Part of her knew she would be expected to, but another part of her wanted to hold onto this perfect moment for a little longer. Hold onto the image of a perfect Fitz a little longer. Generous. Unparalleled. Untarnished. She couldn't bear to see him change into Stevie right before her eyes.

Too bad, she owed him. Right?

'Still want to tell me you don't like it?' he asked mildly, a smile toying with the corners of his mouth. As though he wasn't waiting for her to perform her new duty.

She felt the flush from her cheeks to her very toes.

'That was like nothing I've ever known before,' she croaked.

Which was why she really shouldn't begrudge him.

Elle forced a bright smile to her lips as his head bowed to kiss her neck, ignoring the sensations that were flooding through her anew. Placing her hands flat on his chest, she moved him away and dropped down to her knees, her hands searching for his belt buckle as she went.

'What are you doing?'

His voice was sharper than she'd expected. She forced a pleasant, even tone to her words.

'Returning the favour.'

'No.'

Elle startled as his large hands locked tightly around her wrists and he pulled her back to her feet, forcing her to look at him. His dark look was intimidating.

'But you did it for me.' She frowned uncertainly. 'So now it's my turn.'

'That isn't how it works, Elle.'

She stifled her derision.

'Of course it is.'

Fitz couldn't seriously be saying he didn't expect anything in return. No man would, right?

'I don't know how your past relationships—relationship—worked, but that isn't how it should be.'

His clipped tone caught Elle by surprise, making her insides flutter. *Who exactly was he angry with?* He was almost glowering as he stared into her eyes. It was as though he could see right into her soul and she found she couldn't drag her gaze away. The moment seemed to stretch out into eternity. Finally he broke the silence.

'Sex should never be a chore, Elle. You do things because you *want* to. You don't do them because you somehow feel you *owe* the other person.'

It was astonishing how his words seemed to go straight to the root of her fears.

'But—'

'No. There are no "buts" to that simple truth.'

'You don't…?' Elle swallowed, still not quite certain. 'You don't want me to do that for you?'

'I do not,' he confirmed firmly. 'Not when you don't want to.'

'Part of me does,' she whispered sadly, almost by way of apology. But she was surprised to find that abruptly there was a small part of her that really did want to. She dropped her eyes, afraid that she wouldn't be able to say the words if he was still holding her gaze.

'Because it's you.'

Unexpectedly a soft smile chased the darkness from Fitz's face as he hooked a finger under her chin to force her to look back up at him.

'Then I hope for you that one day someone, the *right* guy, will make more than just a part of you feel that comfortable. But for now I suggest we move over to that bed and I show you other ways we can continue this evening.'

His words were bitter-sweet. The realisation that he really wasn't going to allow this one moment to spoil the rest of the night warred with the reminder that he wasn't her right guy, he was just her one and only tonight guy.

When had she started to forget that?

She managed a jerky little nod, reminding herself not to get so carried away for the rest of the night, ignoring the voice that whispered that Fitz might have been the 'right guy' for her if only she'd been a few months, maybe a year down the road.

The right guy but at completely the wrong time.

'Elle?'

Snapping her head back to the present, she tried to remember the last thing he'd said. Something about moving to the bed to continue their evening.

'I'd like that,' she managed.

With a satisfied nod Fitz dropped his hand from her chin and then, before she could react, he'd taken her hand and was leading her over to the bed.

'Then let's get back to having fun.' He grinned wickedly at her, lowering his head to hers and kissing her as though the ugly moment had never happened.

Incredibly, the further they got from that vestibule and towards the huge inviting bed in the corner the more her mood started to lift. By the time he'd deposited her on the bed, Elle found it easy to kiss him back, some underlying sense of relief lending her a renewed sense of eagerness. As he stood back to finally slide her lacy briefs down, shucking off the last of his own clothing after discreetly throwing a foil square onto the bed, Elle indulged in her first full view of his beautiful physique. He had a stark male beauty that spoke to her very core. And then there was his proud and impossibly generous erection. Her heart flip-flopped and hunger kicked low in her abdomen. Urgent and primal. He was overwhelming, yet he was staring at her as though she was equally breathtaking. As though he were committing every line of her body, every curve to memory.

'Stunning,' he ground out.

His rich, lusty voice seemed to resonate through her very sex, which was still deliciously sensitive after the care he had shown her before. Her long-deflated, crumpled ego began to unfurl and breathe life again.

Tonight might be all they had, but she'd be damned if she wasted it on what-ifs. No, she would thoroughly indulge in every last second of what was left of this night together and then she would hold onto this moment, the memory of this man, for the rest of her life. Pushing herself up onto one elbow, Elle reached for Fitz with a new-found sense of confidence, a warmth spreading though her as he moved onto the bed to join her.

She didn't want to wait another second.

CHAPTER FIVE

FITZ DRANK IN the sight of her, completely naked and laid out on the bed before him looking every bit as enticing and delectable as she had tasted.

'Stunning,' he murmured unconsciously.

God help him, she'd felt better than he'd been imagining all evening. *Hotter, slicker, tighter.* And she was reaching for him as though she couldn't wait any longer.

'We've got all night,' he reminded her, scarcely recognising the raw heat of his own voice.

It was immoral that a woman so bright and sexy and *alive* shouldn't have been lavished every single day with the kind of attention he'd paid to her arresting body, and the realisation that her ex-fiancé had clearly hurt her in this way filled him with inexplicable rage. Yet at the same time Fitz felt an incongruous burst of triumph that *he* should be the one to open her eyes to it. That *he* should have been the one to sweep away her obvious reticence. That *he* had completely erased from her head her unspoken expectation that he'd somehow end up letting her down.

He wanted to take his time, show her more of how it ought to be between two people, even if it was only for one night. But he didn't think he could wait any longer. His erection was so rock-solid it was almost painful. He couldn't remember ever wanting any other woman with such intensity.

She ran her hands over his chest, his sides, his back, exploring every last inch of his torso, and then, her eyes flitting nervously to his, she grazed her nails gently against his skin. Fitz offered a soft groan of appreciation as his mouth fell to plunder hers, and then without warning her hand was moving around to take him in her hand, fitting him to her palm. His groan was instinctive and far more guttural this time, as he flexed against her.

Something seemed to shift in her attitude as she realised the sexual power she had over him. A mischievous glint appeared in her eyes. A hint, perhaps, of the young woman she'd been before something—or someone—had quashed her?

'If we have all night,' she observed, running her thumb around him and then over his tip, 'surely we can slow things down *next* time.'

'You're sure that's what you want?' he managed gruffly.

She lifted her heavy eyelids to look at him, those emerald depths almost black with lust, her breath already shallow and rapid.

'Quite sure.'

He didn't need any further invitation. It took him seconds to open the foil square and roll the condom down his length, ignoring the little voice that taunted him that he'd been so caught up in Elle that he'd only remembered protection when it had fallen out of his pocket as he'd taken off his jeans. The bewitching creature had made him forget the one thing he'd been so fastidious about ever since...well, ever since what had happened with Janine.

The baby he'd never fought for. The baby she had lost at three months because he hadn't taken care of her the way he was supposed to have.

He jerked his head up in frustration. These were the blackest of thoughts he'd locked away in a box over a decade ago, and had thought he'd thrown away the key. The beginnings of memories he didn't want resurfacing, tonight of all nights. He'd slept with his fair share of women over the years and not one of *them* had ever pulled at something deep inside him, the way Elle seemed to.

Angrily, he thrust all thoughts from his head.

Tonight was supposed to be about indulging in a beautiful, intelligent woman. A woman who had made him *crave* her, a woman who seemed to want him with the same dark intensity.

Fitz blocked out his mind and concentrated on Elle.

Gently, he nudged her legs apart and covered her body with his, nestling into her wet heat and revelling in the slickness of their bodies moving over each other. And then he gave in to the aching need and slid inside her.

Sensations rushed him, urging him on. Her soft gasp and low moan only pushed him further but he forced himself to go slowly, to give her a chance to stretch around him, to make sure she was ready. Carefully he moved, languorous slides in and out as he watched her, waiting for her to find his rhythm, to meet him, to match him. Until soon they were moving in perfect synchronicity, and she was arching her hips to draw him in deeper and drive him on. Faster and wilder.

He layered butterfly kisses on her sweetly exposed neck when she let her head fall back, like nectar he had been denying himself for so long. And when he heard her gasp his name, a peculiar sense of euphoria flooded through him. A sense of possession.

As if she were his.

The realisation should have slammed him with more force. It should have set alarm bells clanging wildly in his head. It should have made him feel guilty for beginning this madness. He'd sworn to himself back in the street that whatever it was Elle possessed that seemed to stealthily intrude inside him in a way nothing else ever had, he would control it.

Instead, he was imagining she was *his*. Wondering what it would be like to come back to this strong, characterful, beautiful woman again and again. *Stupid.* Because that could never happen. She could never be his, he had nothing to offer but pain and betrayal. He should never have begun this madness with her. But he hadn't been able to help himself, inexorably drawn to her as though her brilliance, her energy could somehow illuminate the darkness in him.

Then she cried his name a second time and he was lost again, consumed by his need for her. And as her body gripped his and she exploded around him with shudder after shudder of her release, he gave himself up completely to the pleasure of her all around him. Seconds later, he followed.

If this was the start of their night together then he could only wish it would never end. Imagine it would never end. For this one night he could pretend he wasn't damaged, wasn't incomplete, that he was the kind of man who could make a woman like Elle happy in life, not just in bed.

She made him feel like he was more than just a good colonel, a good soldier, a good engineer. Elle made him feel that somewhere deep inside he was good man. And, just this once, he wanted to believe it.

He could deal with the fallout later.

Fitz checked his mobile. Zero-five-hundred. He really should get going, back to barracks. He wasn't required specifically but his visible presence around the barracks would be good for his men's morale, especially for those who hadn't been on operational duty before and especially because this was his new role as their commanding officer.

He eased himself out of the bed, but as he rolled Elle rolled too, as though seeking out his warmth, and so help him he couldn't tear himself away. He didn't want to. He kissed her as she pressed herself against him, his own reaction instantaneous at the feel of her silken skin all along the length of his body.

'I have to leave,' he whispered, making no effort at all to untwine himself from her arms.

'Already?'

Sleepily seductive, she stretched languorously until she realised exactly what she was stretching against. Her eyes flew open wide.

'Morning,' he managed wryly.

She peered at the clock and grumbled good-naturedly.

'Barely. You really have to go?'

'I have time for breakfast.' The words slipped out before his mind had a chance to engage.

'Really?'

No.

'Yes.'

Quickly, quietly she slipped out of bed, unashamedly searching for her clothes as though being with him here the morning after wasn't awkward or strange at all. And he liked it. He liked her confidence, her strength, the certainty that last night hadn't been a mistake.

He pulled his T-shirt over his head, watching as she slipped her feet into tiny ballet pumps from the wardrobe across the room, and then, as she rounded the bed, he reached impulsively for her hand.

'Come on, I know a little bakery nearby. I'll take you there.'

Steadfastly he ignored the part of his brain telling him he should get going. He ignored it as they walked, hand in hand with an intimacy he'd never known before, down the deserted streets. He ignored it as he easily talked his old friend into letting them into the bakery before it was supposed to be open. He ignored it while he listened to Elle's soft voice chatting to him as the early sunlight danced over her animated features and played with the light as it bounced off hair he longed to lose his fingers in again and again. And as she watched him curiously, he couldn't help asking what it was she was thinking.

She hesitated, a shy smile tugging at her lips.

'I didn't think this was what the morning after would look like.' She ducked her head and concentrated on a few crumbs of her almond croissant, unable to meet his eyes.

'What did you expect?' he heard himself asking, as if him leaving wasn't how he'd expected the early hours to unfold either.

'I thought you'd be gone. Sneaking away in the night. You told me you didn't do relationships.'

'I don't.' He took another sip of his black coffee, aware of the irony.

'Yet here you are.' She finally lifted her head. 'You don't seem as emotionally disconnected as you like people to think.'

Her words should have alarmed him. Instead, he felt immeasurably sad.

'You don't know me.'

'So tell me.'

And instead of shutting her down, he thought of the way she'd opened up to him last night. How she'd bravely told him about her sexual experiences with her ex. He'd thrilled in showing her exactly how good it could be, his own body hardening beyond anything he'd ever experienced at the sound of her coming undone in his arms.

Now the words came from nowhere he recognised. A dark place within him that he'd locked down so many years ago, like a kid with a scary monster in the closet. But the light she shone made everything less frightening.

'My father was army, like me,' he began, hesitantly at first. 'Only he wasn't a commissioned officer, he was a nineteen-year-old corporal with his sights set on staff sergeant and beyond when he met my mother. A couple of months later she found she was pregnant and they got married. He always resented being tied down. He took it out on my mother, usually with his fists, usually when he'd been out drinking, although I didn't know about it for years. My mother had always been terrified he'd hurt me so she did the only thing she felt she could, and took the beatings in silence as long as he left me alone, and later my sister.'

'Fitz!' Elle gasped, and tried to disguise it, but Fitz didn't miss her shock. He fought to shut out the memories, so old and repressed they were like a silent black and white movie in his head now. But they still made his heart thump furiously in his chest, like it was trying to ram its way out. Like it was trying to escape.

'Mum and I used to breathe a sigh of relief every time he walked out that door with his kitbag for another tour, especially if he'd been home a while. Him being away meant months of blissful peace, and if we were lucky and he went somewhere else for R&R, we might even get a full year.'

'Were you close, then? You and your mum?' Elle asked gently.

'Sort of.' He hunched his shoulders. No emotions, just facts. He couldn't explain this urge to talk to Elle, just that it was there. But that didn't mean he was ready to actively *think* about it, *feel* it. Not yet.

'But my mother was as unhappy in her own way as he was. Neither of them had wanted to marry the other, but they'd had no choice. Add to that the fact he beat her, and it made for a fairly unpleasant life. I never lacked for anything in terms of food, clothing, toys. She worked hard, and in her own way she loved me, but she was never exactly the huggy sort of mum from American TV shows. It was never a happy home, not exactly full of love.'

'It's all relative, isn't it?' Elle murmured, almost to herself. 'I thought I had it bad with my stepmother, but at least I got to experience something better before that. I knew it didn't have to be that way.'

Fitz shrugged, unable to answer that.

'Maybe. But maybe it's worse. Sometimes words can hurt as much as fists. If someone says you're worthless, stupid, unwanted often enough, you can start to believe them.'

Elle nodded sadly.

'My stepmother was devious. She'd pretend to be okay when my father was around but when he wasn't, she was spiteful and vindictive. If I hadn't had Stevie, if I'd been a bit younger, I might have let her win. In many ways I got lucky, but then it only added to my guilt later for not loving him.'

'He didn't deserve your love.' A stab of jealousy sliced through him.

'But he deserved my honesty.'

'Words are powerful tools in the right hands,' Fitz said slowly. 'But powerful weapons in the wrong ones.'

Elle met his gaze, thoughtful and open.

'Or else they're meaningless,' she countered. 'Stevie used to tell me he loved me, but all the while he was cheating on me. I think I'd far rather have actions over words.'

Fitz nodded but said nothing. He knew he would too, but he hadn't any right to it. He'd always failed in his actions. In trying to be everything his father hadn't been, he'd ended up acting in precisely the same self-serving way. He couldn't escape his nature, it seemed.

'So what happened, Fitz?' Elle touched his arm sadly and Fitz worked to loosen his tightly clamped jaw.

'When I was fifteen he got injured and he was home for a long while. Things just deteriorated. One night, or at least the early hours of the next morning, he came in steaming drunk. I don't know what she said or did, probably nothing, but he completely lost it. I remember hearing her trying to muffle her screams so she didn't wake me or my two-year-old baby sister. Something snapped in me. One minute I was in my bed and the next I was in my parents' bedroom and my dad was lying flat out on the floor and I was threatening to kill him if he ever touched her again.'

Despite the monochrome background of the rest of the memory, he could still see the bright red stain on the dirty carpet from his father's bloodied nose. And the absolute shock on the old man's face.

'He hit you?'

'He didn't dare,' Fitz snorted bitterly. 'A bully doesn't pick on someone he can't intimidate. But he never touched my mother after that. In fact, he pretty much never returned to their army house after that. They stayed married, at least for appearances, but he took posts that meant he was stationed away. He did courses during his downtime, and on the couple of occasions he really didn't have anywhere else to go, my mother took my sister and me to visit her sister, who was married to a soldier and stationed abroad.'

'So you never really saw him again?'

'Not really. He'd never been interested in a family anyway. His wife and son had been imposed on him. My sister was the product of a married couple who went through the motions. So, no, we didn't really see him again. Not until that last time.'

'What happened the last time, Fitz?' Elle half-whispered, as though a part of her already suspected it wasn't good.

He hunched his shoulders, feeling suddenly chilled in the otherwise pleasant late-afternoon air. Suddenly it wasn't easy to tell her anything more. Suddenly, he wished he'd never started. The words were lodged thick and painful, choking in his throat.

'The night he came back was the night they died.'

'The car crash,' she said quietly.

Guilt, anger, grief, all of which had been simmering barely beneath the surface until now, suddenly rushed Fitz so hard he felt physically winded. It took him several long moments to regulate his breathing enough to answer her.

'Yes,' he bit out. 'I don't want to talk about that any more. I don't usually. Last night was the anniversary of their deaths. It's been eighteen years and I realised that I've now been without them, without her, for longer than I ever had her. I guess it just got to me.'

'It would get to anyone!' Elle exclaimed.

'So let's just close it down now and enjoy the last hour or so we have left.'

It wasn't a request and he could see her biting back whatever she'd been about to say.

'Of course,' she said instead.

So they did. Fitz fought to shrug off the unwanted, alien emotions and the acknowledgement that talking to Elle had been far more cathartic than he could ever have imagined. And he let himself enjoy the last hour as they made their way back to the hotel, and to her room, and he couldn't stop himself from making love to her one more time. This time, when he woke he slid carefully out of the bed, seeing her hair puddled on the white pillow like a splash of light, and dressed in silence. Wishing they had more time.

Not knowing what difference that would have made.

He headed for the door, opening it softly to let himself out, before stepping back inside, crossing the room and snatching up a pen and paper from the desk under the mirror and jotting down his phone number.

Last night had been perfect, like a dream he'd never expected to experience. He'd never felt so connected, so at ease with anyone before. But it was just an illusion. A woman he'd met in a bar. For her, he was a means of putting something between her and her failed engagement. For him, a last indulgence before yet another tour of duty. Not that he begrudged it, he loved his career. It was who he was.

Or at least it was the good part of who he was.

Fitz stared at the phone number in his hands. What was he thinking? This hadn't been a first date. Yes, he dated occasionally, but only women who knew the score from the start. Women who agreed from the start. And he ended it as soon as they began to start talking seriously. And for good reason. He was incapable of loving selflessly. He was damaged, and he hurt people. He'd tried to love when he'd found Janine, but even with her he hadn't been able to make that part of his soul work again. Hurting someone as lovely as Elle would be inevitable if he was selfish enough to pursue her. Worse, it was dangerous, because he couldn't shake the feeling that she would challenge every rule he had for himself.

He would never have set aside his meticulously planned schedule of going in early this morning for any other woman. Not for a croissant and a coffee, and not to spend that last hour in their company talking about long-buried emotions.

Ripping the paper from the pad, he screwed it into a tight ball and launched it into the bin, and still he had to force himself to leave Elle's room without a backward glance.

The soft sound of the door closing finally woke Elle. She sat up, the bed sheet clutched tightly to her constricting chest as she stared around the empty suite with fresh eyes. One night with Fitz and now the hotel room, which had felt like a pleasant refuge for the last few nights, suddenly felt cold and lonely.

She felt cold and lonely.

Dropping the sheet and sliding out of the bed,

Elle shook the notion roughly from her head. Last night had been a one-night stand. But as wonderful, as incredible as it had been, it had just been that. One night. No strings. No regrets.

Padding around the suite, Elle forced herself to concentrate on the mundane. To clean her teeth, to get her shower, to dry her hair. But everything felt different. *She* felt different. She sat at the dressing-table mirror and stared at her reflection, almost disappointed that she didn't *look* different too. How could it be that she looked exactly the same as she had last night when inside her it felt as though she had undergone such a seismic shift?

Part of her expected Fitz to walk back in any moment. After the way they'd connected, how was it possible for him to walk away without a second thought? Almost on autopilot, she ran the brush through her hair and chased it with the hair-dryer, trying not to remember with such startling clarity the way Fitz had run his fingers through her hair, telling her how beautiful it was, how beautiful *she* was, bit by bit restoring every bit of confidence that Stevie's actions had knocked out of her. Maybe even more.

Elle wasn't quite sure when or how her brain registered the pen and notepaper, no longer at the back of the table where they'd been her entire stay. Her eyes scanned the room for anything she'd missed but she saw nothing and then, almost instinctively, she glanced over to look into the waste basket. It was empty but for one screwed-up ball of white paper. Her heart slammed inside her chest as she stared, immobile. Slowly, very slowly, she reached out with one trembling hand and retrieved the paper.

Now what?

She willed herself to open it but instead sat, her back ramrod straight, her fingers quivering, gazing at the little white ball, unable to act. It might not say anything. It might say something that would spoil the night before. A tiny voice warned her that she might be better dropping it back in the basket and leaving well alone.

The voice was probably right, but she found she simply couldn't. With painstaking precision she smoothed the page and scanned the phone number, her fingers tracing the letters of his name almost of their own volition.

Then, abruptly, her brain roared into life and she screwed the paper back up.

It was a relief to know that he had felt that same connection she had, and he'd been as seduced by it as she had. But then he'd recognised it for what it was. A snapshot. A perfect moment in a perfect night.

Last night she'd been crazy and impulsive, like a role an actor played for a movie. But that wasn't who she was in real life. She wasn't carefree or daring, she was steadfast and focused, a major, a combat doctor in the British army. However perfect last night had seemed, it had been built on foundations that were little more than illusions, and she couldn't help the stab of guilt at her part in that.

But what was done was done. Last night had been about getting closure on a relationship that had actually died years ago, not about the start of something new. She wasn't ready for that, and she didn't want it. However much Fitz might have confused that for her right now.

Fitz had been right to throw his number away, they would only be chasing after something that didn't really exist. Bracing herself, Elle hurled the paper back into the basket before she could change her mind again.

Last night had been perfect. Trying to squeeze anything more out of it would only sully the wonderful memories she now had. *Just Elle* was gone. It was time to get back to Major Gabriella Caplin, army trauma doctor.

CHAPTER SIX

'THIS IS ARI,' the nurse, a corporal who'd been there a month or so longer than Elle, informed her as soon as she came on shift for the morning. 'He's eight and he has a broken leg with an open wound. This is his first visit to us but the team at the main hospital have been trying to treat him for over a month.'

Elle smiled at the boy, receiving a sweet smile in return as he clung onto his mother's hand. Her own fears were masked by a tight smile, too. The nearest hospital was across the border, several hours and a treacherous drive away. It was no wonder that even though this hospital had been intended to be just a training ground for local doctors, with only a few cases while the army got the rebuild under way, the locals were ignoring that and bringing their sick and injured here anyway.

Another reason why getting this hospital back up and running quickly was so essential.

'They've been trying to heal the infected wound

before they can attempt to set the bone,' the nurse added.

Elle nodded. Infection really was the enemy out here. Even if they set the bone, it wouldn't heal unless the infection was gone.

'He needs a smaller surgical plates-and-pins kit that I don't have among my army kit,' Elle assessed quickly. 'Neither do Razorwire. But our logistics teams are bringing supplies all the time now we're out here, so I'll put in a requisition for more instruments appropriate for dealing with children. In the meantime, we do need to get the infection under control.'

'He can't tolerate washing the wound without anaesthesia,' the nurse warned. 'And we don't have any here.'

'No, well, without the custom-sized plates and pins to hold the bones together they'll be moving and the pain will be incredible for him. We'll leave the leg in plaster for now and wash the wound as much as Ari can withstand, and always under anaesthetic. As soon as the smaller surgical plates arrive we'll be able to hold the bones together and we'll have more options.'

'Understood,' the nurse confirmed.

'Who's in the next bay?'

'Young boy named Zav. He's only five. He suffers from a severe form of thalassaemia so he needs blood transfusions every five weeks. His family are from a village a little east of here, wealthy by local standards, but they say they can't keep making the journey across the border and want to bring him to this hospital for his transfusions.'

'Right.' Elle nodded grimly. Thalassaemia wasn't uncommon out here, not just as an inherited blood disorder, but also because there was no national plan to tackle the disease. It meant that few health facilities could offer treatment for the more severe cases, and parents weren't educated on its causes, which were mutations in the DNA of cells. They only understood the symptoms of chronic fatigue, anaemia and, ultimately, if she recalled rightly, a life expectancy of around fifteen years in this region. Twenty years across the country.

'I take it infection, bone deformities and slowed growth rates, especially in children, are common.'

'Right,' the nurse agreed. 'We see a lot of abnormal bone structure in the face and skull, broken bones, iron overloads and heart problems such as arrhythmias and congestive heart failure.'

Elle nodded. There was little she could say. Treatments were basically frequent blood transfusions or stem-cell transplants, usually from a non-affected sibling. Otherwise, affected or carrier parents would be looking at IVF with embryos pre-tested for genetic defects. Hardly a possibility in a country like this one.

'And in the far bed?' Elle forced herself to move on.

'A two-month-old. Bronchiolitis.'

Again, not uncommon in this region, affecting hundreds of babies every season. Still, she would be glad when the rebuild was under way and she could start kitting out dedicated wards with incubators, paediatric kits and equipment for women in labour. Training the local health professionals to be part-doctors, part-nurses, part-surgeons, however, promised to be no mean feat.

As she flew around the wards—or what passed for wards in the damaged hospital—Elle considered the best place to start in terms of the rebuild. She knew that Major Carl Howes, the officer in command of the troop working at the hospital itself, was focussed on getting the main infrastructure up first. Without water and power, everything else would be doubly hard, but the discovery of an unexpected aquifer running below the area had thrown their programme into turmoil, and Carl

had told her he'd called in his commanding officer to go through the finer details.

She could only hope Carl's colonel was as much
of an expert as Carl claimed the man was.

She glanced quickly at her watch. There was a
joint regiment briefing in a couple of hours and
her own commanding officer had flown in as
well. She really didn't want to keep him waiting
so her ward rounds were going to be postponed.
Grabbing a hat for the shade, Elle ducked outside,
seeing the older man straight away and beaming
at her mentor.

'Colonel Duggan, thanks for flying in. I take it
you've heard about the aquifer?'

Fitz surveyed the vast expanse of nothing beneath
the helicopter as it flew the hour or so trip across
the barren land, his eyes constantly scanning,
more out of habit than anything since they were
in a non-combat environment out here.

Part of him was actually relishing the challenge
of the unexpected aquifer. Anything to occupy his
mind, to distract it from the emerald-eyed, flame-
haired beauty who had haunted his dreams—wak-
ing and sleeping—for almost a week now. He
couldn't shake her from his memory, but every

time he tried to work out what made her so special, so unique from any other woman he'd dated, he just seemed to tie himself up in knots.

It was uncharacteristic and he loathed it. Yet he wouldn't have changed it even if he could have.

He'd watched a group of squaddies playing with a deck of cards the previous night and had realised that right now his life, his career had been like a perfectly ordered deck of cards until Elle had given them a playful shuffle. It had taken him all of the last week to re-order them and fit them neatly back into their box.

Still, he had no intention of letting them get messed up again. Not while he was out here on tour, in any case.

Maybe afterwards, once he returned home, if visions of that flame-haired, emerald-eyed temptress still haunted his dreams, he might consider stepping out of his comfort zone and contacting the hotel to see if he couldn't inveigle something—anything—out of them regarding Elle's name.

Anything to sate the gnawing ache she'd left inside him.

Finally the heli landed, and Fitz stepped out to

greet Major Howes, one of the five majors under his direct command.

'Colonel.'

'Major.'

'How was your ride, sir?'

'Fine, thanks. Good to see you again, Major. We missed each other at Razorwire.'

'Yes, sir, I didn't think I'd have to wait long for you to come out and see the hospital site first-hand. I'm glad, too, as I could use someone with your particular specialism right now. I was going to radio HQ to send me someone yesterday but then I heard you were on your way. I'll show you around when you're ready.'

'I'm happy for you to show me around now,' Fitz said as they moved out of the way while soldiers began unloading the several tonnes of materials and equipment from the heli.

Dutifully, Carl instructed a young lance corporal to take Fitz's pack to his office.

'How was the drive out here?' Fitz asked as the two officers slipped easily into conversation.

The convoy had left Razorwire earlier in the week before Fitz had even arrived. He would have preferred to have travelled with them, it was always good to get an idea of the ground, but he had been needed elsewhere.

'Six hours. Not bad.' Carl shrugged. 'The route was long but that's because we still have to go the long way round that valley, and you know what passes for roads around here.'

'You're lucky if they're paved,' Fitz acknowledged. 'So what's the issue you wanted me here to look at? You mentioned an aquifer.'

'Your speciality. It runs directly beneath where we're planning on putting the plant room for the generators. I had a couple of solutions, which I was going through with the medical liaison officer, but I'd like it if you could run over them, too.'

'Okay, when did you schedule the briefing for me today?'

'Zero-nine-hundred hours. Ninety minutes away.'

'Understood. Then don't let me hold you up, let's go.' He followed as Carl led the way around the hospital, mentally orientating himself as they progressed. 'What's the medical colonel running this hospital like? Colonel Duggan, isn't it? I heard he had a good reputation as a surgeon, don't tell me he's making things difficult on our construction side?'

'No, the Colonel is okay,' Carl answered as they

made their way through and around the part-damaged, part-derelict hospital. 'He *has* got a good reputation apparently, and he mainly deals with teaching the local doctors. But one of the majors under his command, a Major Caplin, has experience both as a combat doctor *and* of building cottage hospitals back in the UK, so her CO has been happy to pass a lot of the liaison work on to her.'

'Makes sense if she has that kind of experience and he doesn't.' Fitz nodded, thinking how he'd always found that one of the greatest strengths of the British army. 'But not if she's insisting the plant room go above the aquifer without considering the other options.'

As structured and hierarchical as it might appear to an outsider, in reality it was far more nuanced and elastic. A brigadier should be willing to take advice from a lieutenant, or even a sergeant, if that individual had specific expertise that everyone else lacked. For all intents and purposes, he could be answerable to this Major Caplin if her commanding officer Colonel Duggan had passed over administrative and operational command of the hospital rebuild to her. Usually, it worked well and was balanced. But if she was awkward and demanding the hospital be constructed in a way that wasn't feasible then he was prepared to pull rank if required.

'No, she isn't insisting that. She's tough and she knows what she wants, but she also has a good head on her shoulders and she isn't difficult to work with. She's clearly a skilled doctor, too.'

Fitz eyed his old friend shrewdly.

'She's also attractive, isn't she?' he noted wryly. 'I'd forgotten you were one for the females.'

'Only single commissioned females. Usually back home but certainly never in a combat zone,' Carl pointed out with a sheepish grin. 'I'm always discreet and I don't contravene the rules. I *never* dip into the non-commissioned officers pool. I value my career, thanks. Besides, there's no need for us all to be complete monks like you.'

He'd either forgotten about Janine, or deliberately wasn't mentioning her. Janine's father—back then a colonel, now a general—had no doubt made sure of that.

Lost in his own thoughts, Fitz was completely unprepared when he rounded the corner.

Just Elle?

Shock stole over him, taking his breath and leaving him feeling physically winded. She might as well have snatched that perfectly ordered deck of cards he'd imagined earlier out of his hands and hurled them high into the cloudless sky. Now some were fluttering in the breeze while others plummeted, ominously, to land face down in the dust.

Even putting one foot in front of the other suddenly seemed like a mammoth feat.

She couldn't be out here. The woman, the one-night stand he was already struggling to put behind him. Surely it was impossible now?

And yet he *had* to put that night behind him. *Especially now.*

Oblivious, Carl stepped forward and made the formal introductions.

'Colonel Fitzwilliam, this is the medical CO, Colonel Duggan. And one of the majors under his command, Major Caplin.'

'Fitz,' he clarified, holding his hand out to his counterpart, focussing on the older man. But the only person he could see, could focus on, was Elle.

'Phil,' Colonel Duggan responded immediately.

A solid handshake and warm greeting confirmed Carl's assessment of the guy as a secure

CO. It was all Fitz could do to keep his eyes from sliding to the side.

But even in his peripheral vision he could see how remarkably stiff Elle was, blood draining from her face to leave two pinched high spots. He got the sense that if she'd been allowed to salute in the field, she would have. Evidently she was as thrown as he was, yet Fitz was helpless against the inexplicable sense of anger welling inside him.

He prided himself on his focus, his drive, his steadiness. And Elle threatened all that. She made him feel unbalanced. He *allowed* her to unsettle him and he didn't know who he was more furious with.

He was only grateful that army protocol gave him some semblance of structure that he might otherwise have felt was lacking.

'Major.'

'Colonel.' She thrust out her hand to take his with no acknowledgement in her expression.

Yet there was no doubting the spark that arced between them as their hands made contact, the hitch in her breath as it grew shallow, the way his chest pounded. Things that only the two of them would notice, but which proved the attraction from that night hadn't dimmed in any way.

If anything, it seemed to have increased.

He had to act. Before she did something stupid like pretend they'd never met. They might not be about to flaunt the exact circumstances of their encounter—that wasn't anyone else's business but their own—but neither did it mean it was anything they should need to hide.

Ignoring the voice in his head challenging why he *really* didn't like the idea of going along with it—the inexplicable sense of possession—Fitz smothered his irrational fury and dipped his head.

'We've already met. Once. Isn't that right, Major?'

She managed a murmur of agreement but he had already turned back to his counterpart. As though that would somehow ground him, as though the more professional he could keep it, the less he could pretend he was affected by her. Until he'd managed to control his frustration.

'Major Howes informs me there's already been a development. An aquifer that wasn't previously identified?'

'That's right,' Colonel Duggan agreed. 'Directly beneath the intended location for the medical gas supply system.'

'But it shouldn't be too much of an issue.' Fitz frowned. 'We can bridge over it or close it in.'

The medical colonel held a hand up with a smile.

'Let me stop you there, Fitz. Major Caplin here has experience in hospital construction so it's better if she runs you through her concerns. My expertise is as a vascular surgeon and I'm mainly based at the field hospital back in Razorwire, so Major Caplin essentially has administrative and operational command of this hospital. Of course, she keeps me updated in her daily sit-rep so I'm always happy to discuss it with you, but it might be easier to speak to the major in the first instance.'

Just what he didn't need.

'Not a problem, Phil.'

'Then, if you'll excuse me, I've got a teaching operation scheduled in about half an hour. I'll send someone to let you know when I'm out and we can go through anything.'

'Appreciate it,' Fitz confirmed, as the man checked with Elle if she needed anything else.

He couldn't blame the man, it was exactly what he would have done. In fact, hadn't he left his second-in-command liaising with brigade back at Razorwire in his absence? Furthermore, Carl was right, Colonel Duggan looked like he would be good to work with. The man was secure enough to acknowledge when it was advantageous to hand off to his more experienced major, but still remain directly responsible.

If only that major wasn't Major Caplin, wasn't Elle. Not that he didn't respect her or admire her—far from it. But he couldn't imagine working with someone whose laugh still jingled in his head and whose body he could taste on his tongue if he closed his eyes.

'Nice to meet you, Colonel,' Colonel Duggan signed off cheerily, and Fitz forced himself back to reality with a pleasant smile.

'Likewise.'

With the medical CO gone, that left him and Carl. And Elle. With Carl gazing at her with respect and a hint of lust, which only an old friend like Fitz himself would have recognised.

Something shot through him. Something which—if he hadn't known better—he might have mistaken for a touch of jealousy and…possession?

But he did know better.

He knew because he'd sworn, after Janine, that he'd never allow himself to blur the lines between personal and professional again. And now that Elle was out here, with him, in this environment, he *had* to stop remembering that night.

He liked things to be distinct, clear, compartmentalised. It avoided messiness.

He didn't date army colleagues. Oh, there was no rule against him and Elle getting together that night, but it was a line he didn't like to cross in his own mind. Just as he didn't *do* long-term relationships.

He wasn't built for them. He was too selfish. Too thoughtless. Too damaged.

The kind of man who'd been too busy celebrating his eighteenth with his mates to take the time out to listen to his voicemail. For the sake of thirty seconds, he'd have heard his mother's desperate, frightened message. Their deaths were on his hands.

The one time he'd thought he could be a better person, he'd thought he could be there for Janine the way he never had been for his family, he'd failed again. The loss of their unborn baby, another death on his conscience.

He couldn't run from it. It was in his DNA.

A good soldier. A good leader.

A destructive family man.

One-night stands and temporary relationships with women who never knew the military side of him meant he never had to deal with complications when they ended. He'd been meticulous about keeping the two sides of his life distinct from each other.

And now here he was. Acutely aware of the woman standing stiffly beside him. A woman who had made him feel the most relaxed and comfortable that he'd been in a long, long time. That night with her he'd actually felt a carefree happiness.

But wanting something more with Elle now, as a fellow officer, would allow his personal life to bleed into his professional one, a no-go in his mind. Or at least it *should* have been a no-go. Yet even now, as his initial shock dulled, he couldn't shake the possibility. As if Elle had the ability to break down whatever barriers he tried to erect between them.

He'd never felt so off-kilter. Elle had sneaked under his skin when he hadn't noticed and all he could think of was how she'd looked in his arms, how she'd tasted when he'd kissed her, and how she'd sounded when he'd made her come apart time and again.

He was hardly surprised when Elle jumped straight in with a determinedly professional expression. And then her eyes locked with his and there was no doubting that she was as unsettled as he was. Both of them striving to remain soldier-like, both of them unable to help homing in on each other as though it was just the two of them in the whole world.

'I understand from Major Howes that the soil on either side of the aquifer is hard and competent, so it might be possible to bridge it. However, he did mention he wanted to get advice from an aquifer specialist. I didn't know that was you, *sir*.'

Fitz doubted Carl would hear anything but polite respect in her tone. But, then, Carl hadn't got to know the major quite as intimately as he himself had.

'Major Howes is right. It is possible to bridge some aquifers, but I'd need to study this one before I could confirm it in this case. I don't know what the pressure is in the aquifer, and even if the soil either side is hard and competent, if it's made up of over-consolidated silt it could wash away if we have to drive any piles into the ground.'

'He mentioned basal uplift?'

Why wasn't he surprised that Elle had absorbed every bit of information Carl must have given her? And, just like when they'd pulled together so harmoniously back at the bar with the young lad and his sister, Fitz found himself slipping easily back into working with her. Setting aside their unsettled history for the moment.

'That can happen if we excavate the water and soil from on top of the aquifer—which is currently keeping it contained—and the pressure within the aquifer itself bursts, swamping this entire site. That could also happen even if we don't have a blow-out but simply pierce the aquifer.'

'That sounds like a risk we don't want.' She frowned.

'Only if we don't allow for it. We can drill a series of relief wells, even back-up relief wells, and instal pumps to get some draw-down and relieve the pressure. We can also spread the footings of the buildings to avoid piles piercing the aquifer.'

'And what if we moved the plant room altogether, how feasible is that?'

'It depends how extensive the aquifer is. Major Howes and I have already agreed this is a priority discussion.'

'If at all possible, I'd like to consider moving to the other side of the site, to avoid any risk of contaminating the aquifer altogether,' Elle stated firmly. 'In this area the population mainly use groundwater, either from foothill infiltration or from riverbed exfiltration, with little chance of rainwater recharge. And with the population in this region growing exponentially, there is increasing over-exploitation of the scarce water resources.'

He could see exactly where she was heading.

'So you want to tap into this aquifer for the local communities. Perhaps a series of clean water wells?'

'I'm not a ground surveyor like you are, and I certainly don't know anything about aquifers to speak of, but I would think this offers a significant clean water supply to the community, especially when cholera and other water-borne diseases are so prevalent out here. Do you agree, Colonel?'

'I do,' he mused, looking over her shoulder at the basic geological plans Carl had already put together. 'But if you're moving across the site, it will mean redesigning your hospital layout. The main hospital itself, as damaged as it has been over the last decade, is still the best medical resource the local population have.'

The familiar citrusy scent powered into him before he realised it, tightening his chest and stealing his breath away.

'So we need to minimise the impact on them

and make as few alterations as possible. Yes, Colonel,' Elle bit out, stiffening abruptly.

Their sudden proximity clearly affected her just as much as it did him. Fitz jerked around to Carl, as much to remind himself of his Major's presence as anything else.

'Any ideas, Major Howes?'

'Working on it, sir.' Carl stepped forward, apparently unaware of the tension Fitz felt was practically sparking between himself and Elle. 'The plant room houses the heat, ventilation and air-conditioning units.'

Fitz made a quick assessment.

'Which means also moving the generators in the next-door unit since they'll be relying on the HVAC plant room to keep them cool, especially in these temperatures.'

'What about moving the medical gas supply system here?' Elle tapped another location on the map, and he stepped close again, so close her fingers accidentally brushed his and his gut kicked in response even as she snatched her hand away.

'The HVAC could go here—' the faint, almost imperceptible quiver in her voice betrayed her '—and the generators could go there.'

'What's on that side of the wall?'

'The ICU.'

'Then no. And, anyway, I'd like the generator-housing unit to have bigger blast walls if we're having to move them closer to the hospital.' Fitz scanned the ground. 'Can we take a walk around? I've studied the plans back at Razorwire, and I had a good aerial view coming in, but I want to see it for myself.'

'Colonel.' Elle and Carl acquiesced simultaneously.

He was used to it, a first-name basis in private but generally formal in public, yet this time it particularly reminded him of how well he and Elle had worked together before. How effortlessly they'd slipped into working together now. How easy she made it.

At every turn she challenged his fears of complications and messiness. She made him wonder whether he could have more after all. More time with her. More *of* her.

The possibility intrigued him.

And the distraction annoyed him.

Forcing himself to focus on the plans in front of him as well as the geography of the site, Fitz tried to forget that Elle was suddenly *here*, and concentrated on mapping it all in his head. It was a sixty-bed hospital, with electricity intermittent. So the back-up generators were vital, as was good access from the road to fuel them. He moved around the site thoughtfully, finally coming back to a possibility in his mind.

'So the proposed ORs were to have been on the other side of this wall?'

'Yes.' Elle nodded. 'On each side of the corridor.'

Fitz consulted the design then glanced over the other end of the site, warming to his work as he always did, and forgetting for a moment that he and Elle had any issues between them.

'So, hypothetically, if we extended that part of the facility to house them on the other side, we'd have to move the recovery areas too?'

'Yes. And building room is tighter on this side so, as you said, we'd have to either create more space between the hospital and the proposed location for the generators, or build thicker blast walls.'

'It could work,' Fitz mused. 'I need to look into it in more detail and understand how your internal layout for the hospital works.'

He'd built plenty of bridges, railheads, electricity plants and more in his time, not to mention demolished or blown up a fair few buildings. But this was the first hospital he'd built.

'I admire your frankness, Colonel.' Elle beamed unexpectedly when he told her as much, and a thousand explosions went off in Fitz's chest, like an unused pyrotechnics display at the end of an army year.

It was impossible not be drawn into those vivid emerald pools.

And that smile.

It was ridiculous that he'd been missing that smile so profoundly. He didn't miss smiles. He didn't miss people.

She made him feel things he'd never felt before and he couldn't afford that. The last time he'd tried to pretend that he was normal, that he wasn't missing fundamental pieces of a human being, he'd ended up causing immeasurable pain. He could still recall the distraught expression on Janine's face, the pain, the hurt, the recrimination in her eyes when she'd screamed at him that she'd have been better off never meeting him in the first place.

He was broken, and his attempts to fix himself had only ever caused more pain to those around him.

He was only here for a few days. How hard could it be to keep himself at arm's length from

Elle? To refuse to allow himself to give into temptation and seek her out as though that night had been more than it had been?

'Colonel.' Carl's voice interrupted his thoughts. 'The briefing you scheduled is due to start in forty minutes.'

Had they been that long walking around the place?

'Right.' He jerked his head, forcing himself to focus. 'Thank you, Major.'

'If you don't need me here, I'll go and start setting up, sir.'

'That'll be fine,' Fitz confirmed smoothly, watching Elle twist her hands in discomfort.

This was the moment to put into practice what he'd been thinking. To keep himself at arm's length. To walk away. To let Elle walk away.

He didn't move.

Neither did Elle.

They both knew what was coming. It was inevitable. And unavoidable. They'd fallen into working together with incredible ease but they couldn't ignore their shared night. And, worryingly, he found he didn't want to. So much for it being a one-night stand; he needed to hear her talk about it, to know that she found it as unforgettable as he did. Which only made him all the more irritable.

Fitz waited until Carl had rounded the corner before he began speaking.

'You told me you weren't military.'

'No, I didn't.' She shook her head miserably. 'I told you I was a doctor, I omitted to say I was an army trauma doctor.'

'Yet you knew I was a colonel in the army.'

What was wrong with him that he was blaming her?

It was as though the more frustrated he felt at his own inability to walk away from her, the angrier he felt, and he turned it onto her in some misplaced effort to keep his distance. To stop himself from hauling her into his arms and kissing her senseless. Which, at this instant, was the only thing he ached to do.

Ached.

He'd never wanted anyone like this. Never. It made no damned sense.

'Yes, but I didn't think it would matter.' She swallowed hard. 'Listen, I understand this isn't the most ideal development to our...one-night stand.'

His whole body balked at the sound of the words on her lips. It was *exactly* what that night had

been and yet, ludicrously, it seemed a wholly in-
adequate description.

The ache became a crushing need, the likes of
which he'd never experienced.

'*Not the most ideal development* hardly even be-
gins to describe what this is, wouldn't you agree?'

In his effort to stay distant his voice sounded
harsher, uglier than he'd like, and she jerked her
head up in shock. But he was fighting to make
sense of the maelstrom in his head. In his chest. He
suspected that if he didn't push her away he might
end up kissing her. And he could hardly do that.

'Not ideal, no,' she agreed slowly, tightly. 'But
you're acting like it's a scourge on you or something. It isn't. We haven't contravened a single
rule. We're both commissioned officers and you
aren't my boss. There's no rule against us having
slept together.'

'Not here,' he silenced her, glancing hastily
around, his tone even more brusque than the jerk
of his head.

There was no one about but, still, it didn't hurt
to be careful. He strode angrily back to the set of
buildings, barely pausing to throw a final command over his shoulder.

'My office.'

CHAPTER SEVEN

THERE WAS NO mistaking the barely restrained fury in his glower. Wordlessly she followed him to the main building, her heart detonating in her chest.

Guilt poured through her.

Wait, was he somehow blaming her for the unforeseeable turn of events?

Disappointment crashed over her, almost painful as it burned within her chest and swamped out everything else. All of the fantasies she'd so absurdly cradled this past week, all of her memories, were torn down in a single instant.

What a fool she was, building him up in her head into a perfect, unrealistic image of a man who had shown her such generosity and selflessness that night together, faultlessly anticipating her needs, and then exceeding them, over and over again.

In that one night he'd restored her confidence in herself as a desirable woman. A confidence which had been quashed for so many years—if she'd ever really had it at all. She supposed, whatever happened from here, she should hold onto that memory and be grateful to him for at least such a gift.

Instead, faced with this furious side of Fitz, she wished that night really *had* been all she had. At least that memory would have remained intact. Unblemished by this moment.

Lost in her thoughts, she barely noticed when he stopped without warning, and she ran into the back of him before she could stop herself.

'My office?' he demanded, this time less of an order and more of a question.

He was clearly irritable that he didn't yet know his way around and, for some reason, that made her feel a little more in control of her skittering emotions.

Yes, all right, perhaps she should have told him she was an army doctor, but how could she possibly have known that Fitz would be the commanding officer of the squadron sent to work alongside a unit from the field hospital? Even so, indignation followed the guilt. He had no right to be so arrogant, as though sleeping with her was a black mark on his reputation.

Still, Elle schooled her thoughts, and her voice, determined not to let him see how much he affected her until she'd worked out exactly what it was she was going to say. For now, she'd resume a professional façade and get him back to his office, and then she'd get as far away from him as was possible in this confined place and try to regroup.

'Your office is this way, *Colonel*,' she emphasised.

Carefully, she manoeuvred past him and strode through the rabbit warren of old, partially damaged corridors, all of which looked the same, with none of her usual tour guide fun. Privately she decided she might even get a tiny, perverse kick out of seeing him get lost for the first couple of days. Finally, she stopped outside a nondescript door.

'Your office, Colonel. The stairs are just there.' She waved to the recess behind her. 'And your sleeping quarters are first floor up and the third door down. Two doors down from mine. Although *sleeping quarters* makes them sound a lot grander than the bare concrete cell-like boxes which they actually are. This place is so rundown there isn't a single one that hasn't fallen into disrepair.'

At least, being a colonel, he had a room to himself while she shared with two other female majors, neither of whom were medical and who she didn't know well enough to relax around.

Despite her admonishments to herself it seemed that the wicked streak Fitz had revealed in her had chosen this moment to reassert itself. Even as a delicious memory rippled through her, Elle mentally kicked herself for allowing Fitz to see precisely how he'd inveigled his way into her subconscious.

'Come in and close the door behind you,' he ordered, heading straight into his office and moving to the ancient, steel-framed industrial desk in the far corner. 'I don't want anyone overhearing our conversation.'

His brittle tone sliced through her, so cold it wounded Elle far more than any words could have done. She jutted her chin out, determined not to let herself lose what little ground she'd made on her self-confidence.

'Is there any need for conversation, *Colonel*?' she emphasised again. 'I think we should just forget that night ever happened. It's only for a couple of days, surely, while you check on your squadron out here, and then you'll be back in Razorwire?'

'Is that why you thought pretending we'd never met was such a bright idea, *Elle*?'

The emphasis of her name made it clear he intended to have this out with her. There was little point in continuing any charade. She exhaled a little shakily.

'I thought it was the easiest solution. I've never been in this situation before.'

'Neither have I,' he bit out. 'But I know that other officers saw us together that night. If we stick as close to the truth as possible then we can't get caught out with people assuming there must have been more to it than there was.'

She couldn't help that his words stung a little, as though the idea that it could have been more was preposterous. But at least the surprise admission that he hadn't been in this situation before made her feel a little better. So there wasn't a line of female officers he'd also slept with.

'Fitz, is there really any need for this conversation? I think we both know what you're going to say.'

'Is that so? And what would that be?'

Elle pursed her lips. It was what they'd both agreed that night in the hotel.

Yet somehow it didn't make it any easier.

'That we agreed what we had was a…a one-

night stand. That neither of us could have anticipated we'd end up work colleagues.'

'Couldn't we?' he cut in abruptly. The chillness
in his tone seeped through to her bones despite
the forty-degree heat.

Elle tightened her arms around her body, as
though to offer herself support.

'Say again?'

'Did you really have no idea who I was? I told
you I was a colonel in the Royal Engineers and
that we were deploying. Razorwire was an obvious possibility, you must have put two and two
together.'

'Actually,' Elle shocked herself by interrupting
haughtily, 'you originally said you and your bud-
dies were on a leaving do, and it was only after
I challenged you about the army-issue trousers
you gave that lad after he had that seizure that
you told me you were a colonel, otherwise I doubt
you would have said a word. And you certainly
never mentioned you were Royal Engineers. If
you're going to berate me then you should at least
be accurate.'

She didn't quite recognise the look that danced
over his striking features. And then it was gone
and he was back to chastising her.

'Fine, then for the sake of *accuracy*,' he under-scored, his jaw locked in disapproval, 'you still deliberately concealed the fact that you were an army doctor. Nor, when I told you I was being deployed, did you admit that you were in the middle of your own deployment.'

Elle sucked in a sharp breath. When he put it that way it *did* look bad, but then she already knew that, and while she was prepared to hold her hands up to some of it, she'd be damned if she was going to take the blame for the part for which she was actually innocent.

'You're right. I knew you were an army colonel and I knew you were leaving on a tour of duty, but I didn't say anything. For that, I'm sorry. In my defence, though, how could I possibly have guessed we'd end up in the same place? It isn't like I knew *where* you deploying to. It could have been different areas, different regions, even different countries.'

'Razorwire's a big camp. Plenty of soldiers end up there, you knew it was a possibility,' he bit out, his glare hurled at her with all the pinpoint accuracy of a top athlete throwing a javelin.

Rooted in place, Elle had no choice but to stand

her ground, but she knew she was clinging to very shaky distinctions. Still, they were all she had.

'But we aren't actually *at* Razorwire, are we? I couldn't have foreseen that.'

'You lied to me.'

'No,' she began, then stopped abruptly. 'Maybe.'

Elle exhaled heavily, the fight unexpectedly sucked out of her. He was right. She *had* lied to him. Not for the reasons he assumed, but if they were to work efficiently together for the remainder of her tour, then they were going to need some kind of trust.

And he certainly didn't trust her right now.

'Fitz, I honestly didn't intend to deceive you but I really didn't want to talk *green*, or compare tours, or analyse postings. I didn't want to be Major Gabriella Caplin, heck, I didn't even want to be Elle Caplin that night. Like I told you, I'd just left my ex-fiancé who'd been cheating on me and I wanted one night—just one—where I did something a little crazy and out of character. Something Major Caplin would *never* have done.'

The silence was so thick, so cloying that Elle felt like she was suffocating.

'But, at the risk of repeating myself, you're acting as though it's a big deal when it doesn't have to be. We were perfectly entitled to sleep with each other and even now there's no conflict of interest.'

'I'm a colonel,' he bit out, for the first time appearing less sure of himself.

It might be only the merest hint of a chink in his impermeable armour but Elle wasn't about to let that stop her.

'But you're not *my* colonel,' she pointed out. 'You're not *my* CO. Colonel Duggan is. So a relationship between you and me isn't against the rules, but of course you already know that. So what's this about, Fitz?'

She eyed him speculatively. The look of fury in his black eyes didn't make any sense. Quickly, she ran through anything she might be missing.

'Colonel Duggan has administrative and operational command for the running of this hospital, and therefore *I* do when he leaves the site. You have operational command for the construction of the hospital, and therefore Major Howes does when you're not here. You can't re-task me, or tell me how to do my job. And it's not even a combat environment—we're on a peacetime hearts-and-minds mission, so it isn't as though things could suddenly get hostile.'

'It crosses a line,' he ground out.

'Which line?' She threw up her hands, exasperated.

And then an almost paralysing nausea snaked through her mind. She could barely bring herself to ask the question, but she knew she had to.

'Unless you're not single.' The words tasted acrid on her tongue. 'If you're married then it would have crossed a line, it would have contravened army rules.'

'Of course I'm not married,' he bit out instantly.

Elle grabbed the back of the chair, relief making her knees wobble. After what Stevie had done, she couldn't have endured to be the other woman herself. She couldn't have withstood the idea that Fitz had made her that person.

'So which line?' she repeated shakily.

His pulse leapt beneath his jaw. Evidence, not that she needed it, of his irritation. But she couldn't step back; he'd started this personal attack and now she had to know.

'*My* line,' he spat out, at length.

She had no idea whether his disgust was at her or himself.

'I have my professional life and I have my personal one, and I don't blur the lines between the two.'

Why not?

The question lingered. It was on the very tip of her tongue. Yet she couldn't bring herself to ask it. He would fob her off and she didn't want him to do that. He was clearly one of those soldiers who left his civvy life at the door of the barracks and put on his colonel-soldier one and she could understand that, it was usually how she liked to be on operations, especially if she was going into a combat environment. But out here, on this particular mission, things were more relaxed and Fitz didn't need to be quite so rigid. He wasn't protecting anyone.

Except, perhaps, himself.

Should she leave? Stay? She glanced at Fitz, hoping for some kind of response but he was only watching her. Judging her. For not being able to draw a line the way he could.

She bristled and turned to the door, faltered, then stepped back to his desk.

'You have no right to judge me, you don't even know me.'

'I'm not judging you,' he argued. 'I'm trying to protect you.'

'From whom?' she exclaimed. 'From you?'

The bleak look in his eyes caught her off guard. A haunted look that clawed at her insides.

'Fitz, why on earth would you think I need protection from you?'

He shook his head, his lips pulled into a thin line as though he didn't intend to answer. And then he spoke.

'You're bright and vibrant and happy. And I'll destroy it. It's who I am.'

Incredulity spread through her. That was so far removed from the man she'd met that night.

'Why on earth would you say that?'

He shook his head as though he didn't want to say any more but the words kept coming.

'Because I've done it before. Because I'm my father's son.'

This was about the car crash, she realised with a rush, remembering what Fitz had told her that night. Now she realised he felt guilty over his mother's death. Whether he realised it or not, he was likely punishing himself for still being alive while his mother and sister were gone.

She should have seen it earlier, she should have

recognised it. *Guilt*. She knew it only too well. Only in her case it was guilt and gratitude. Without Stevie she doubted she would ever have realised her dream of becoming a doctor; she simply couldn't have afforded the university course. It was the reason she'd ignored the little signs that Stevie had been cheating on her for a long time. She'd told herself that it wasn't true, and she'd allowed herself to believe it, until that night she'd said the words out loud to Fitz and realised how unlikely they sounded.

And she couldn't shake the suspicion that it was some form of guilt that made Fitz shut people out, deny himself happiness. As though, somehow, he didn't deserve it.

She stepped towards him, shaking her head gently.

'Your father was a drunk. You were a seventeen-year-old kid. What happened to your mother and sister wasn't your fault.'

He laughed—a humourless bark that splintered inside her.

'You have no idea what was or wasn't my fault.'

'So tell me,' she encouraged softly.

She could actually see the battle raging inside him, etched into every chiselled groove of his face. Some part of Fitz wanted to tell her, she was sure of it. But he was fighting it and she didn't know why.

Still, she forced herself to wrinkle her nose at him coolly. As though her every fantasy since last week hadn't involved Fitz doing deliciously wicked things to her.

And then he said the words she least wanted to hear and it felt as though her heart was shattering. Shredded by shrapnel as if it had been caught in a homemade IED.

'After all, it was just sex, right?'

The root of the pain was so deep she couldn't have pinpointed it if she tried. It snatched her breath away and left her legs feeling weaker than those of a newborn foal.

As though it would have been no hardship to him at all to walk away from her that night. When she knew she would have never been able to re-sist him.

Fitz was supposed to have been a one-night stand yet somewhere along the line she'd given him the power to hurt her as much as Stevie had because they were both able to dismiss her as in-consequential.

She tried to steel herself, desperately trying not

to show Fitz how much that throwaway line had hurt her. But she wasn't fast enough, and she felt too raw.

'God, how do you guys *do* that?' she demanded, her voice little more than a strained whisper.

'Elle…'

He took a step towards her but she backed up, shaking her head, unable to get the words out. Unable to process the inexplicable pain.

This had to be about Stevie. It couldn't be about Fitz, that didn't make sense, he had been just a one-night stand. *Stevie* was the one who had hurt her, betrayed her, made her feel worse than nothing. She was just transferring to Fitz because he was here and her ex wasn't.

Right?

Damn Stevie.

She hated him for making her feel like she somehow wasn't enough. Not sexy enough, not available enough, just not enough. And she hated herself for not being able to act cool and nonchalant. For letting Fitz see how vulnerable she still was. She tried to fight back, to claw back some measure of dignity.

'Don't think this is about you,' she choked out between the unattractive barks of bitter laughter.

'I know that.'

She wasn't prepared for the bleakness, the hollowness of his response. As though he really believed her. As though he hadn't for one minute considered the impact he'd made on her.

Caught up in the emotions roiling inside her, she let her neck fall back to stare at the rough-textured grey concrete ceiling and exhaled hard, her head struggling to make sense of it.

This was a side to Fitz she knew for a fact that no one else saw. His reputation preceded him. A fearsome soldier, an inspiring leader, a caring commander. They didn't know the internal war he waged. Hadn't he told her things that he'd said he'd never told anyone else?

Surely that had to count for something?

'But you still can't treat me like the enemy,' she said tentatively. 'I didn't set out to deceive you.'

There had been something between them that first night. A connection that had gone beyond simple attraction, or sex, though both had helped. They'd both confided in each other, and whether it was the events of that evening, the fact that they'd never expected to meet again, or just the fact that her guard had been lowered and he'd been there, Elle couldn't be sure. But they'd opened themselves up to each other and they couldn't just slam those doors shut now because it was no longer convenient.

'I know that too.' He pulled himself up taller, as though regrouping. 'And I know you're not the enemy. I didn't mean to hurt you with what I said. For what it's worth, it isn't personal. I just don't like to have a crossover between my professional life and my private one.'

'What you mean is that you don't like people knowing too much about you, and certainly not the things you told me that night,' she pushed bravely.

It was how she'd intended that night to go, but deep down she suspected it was that shared vulnerability that had allowed her to sleep with him in the first place. She couldn't have gone through it with anyone else but Fitz. It hadn't just been about the sex, as incredible as that had undeniably been, it had been about the way Fitz had made her feel about herself. After Stevie's betrayal had left her feeling so worthless, Fitz had made her feel good about herself again, and he'd made her laugh out loud.

When was the last time Stevie had made her laugh?

'Maybe,' he answered carefully.

'But I know because you told me, and that un-settles you, doesn't it?'

'Elle...' His low voice held a warning, but some reckless facet of her personality, the one that Fitz himself had been the one to awaken, was taking over her.

'Is it because I make it harder for you to take off your *Fitz* head and put on your CO head?' She was proud of herself for keeping the shake out of her voice. 'Or is it because you're still attracted to me?'

Who was this daring, challenging person? She wanted to think this new, bolder side of herself was a reaction to Stevie. Yet somehow it was less about her ex-fiancé and more about Fitz, the man who had made her feel as though he had her back if she needed him, without eroding her own sense of control or undermining her capability.

Elle snapped her head back to see Fitz had ad-vanced on her, closing the gap between them, and for a moment she wondered if he was about to throw her out of his office.

'I think you know the answer to that one.' Fitz's voice rumbled right through her, down to her very core.

Elle couldn't answer. He was close, so close

she could breathe in that all-too-familiar woodsy scent. He was right, she still wanted him as much as she had that night.

Fitz had made her feel wicked and wanton, and all woman. And suddenly Elle wanted to experience that again. If only once more. She tried telling herself it was a fantasy that would never happen, but instead she opened her mouth again. Breathy and seductive and nothing like her usual self.

'I do. So what are we going to do about it?'

CHAPTER EIGHT

HE SHOULD STOP THIS.

He *had* to stop this.

He wanted to pull away but he couldn't, he was rooted to the very spot. Her husky, seductive tone scraped inside him, through him, along his very sex.

It was why he'd closed the gap between them in a move that was infinitely more dangerous than he'd thought. He was drawn to her like a planet to the sun, just as he'd been that night. But it was an illusion. He'd been plagued by ghosts that night, the anniversary of his mother's death, and he'd been looking for something, anything to fill that void and help him stuff back the pain. If it hadn't been Elle, it would have been someone else. The connection they felt wasn't real.

And yet, however many times he told himself that, Elle was all too real.

Which had been part of the magic of that night.

'You were going to leave me your phone number

the next morning,' she breathed, playing it like it was her trump card. Which, he supposed, it was. 'I know you wrote it on the hotel notepad before throwing it in the bin.'

He couldn't answer. There was no response that wouldn't confirm everything she already thought. That one night hadn't been enough.

'It was a mistake. That night was all we could have.'

'So tell me to stop,' she whispered. 'And I'll walk out of here and we won't ever speak of it again, if that's what you want.'

He couldn't even bring himself to open his mouth. The way she was staring at him now, so intently, was infinitely better than the way she'd been watching him a few moments earlier. With such an expression of hurt clouding her lovely features that he felt like a complete coward. He hadn't felt that way since Janine's father had ordered him to get out of their house and never return—and he'd been only too happy to oblige.

That was why he didn't get involved. He let people down, he betrayed them. He hurt people. One look back on his past proved it.

He didn't need Elle as further evidence.

And then he'd given himself away and she'd realised it was all a show, she'd seen exactly how rattled he was.

He'd never been rattled before Elle had come along.

The relief on her face had fired everything back up inside him. Seeing how much it mattered to her, that their one-night stand hadn't been meaningless.

But that didn't mean it was *meaningful* either, and that was the problem. He couldn't offer her a future. Even if he wanted to, he lacked the ability; it wasn't the kind of man he could ever be.

'What do you want from me, Elle?' he rasped.

He didn't know whether he was challenging her because if she couldn't say the words then it gave them an out, or because he so urgently wanted to hear them from her lips.

She swallowed.

'One more night.'

One more night. Not a relationship. Not a future. It seemed like such a reasonable demand, and one his whole being ached to consent to.

He'd never wanted any woman the way he'd wanted her from the moment he'd seen that damned thumb-lock. He'd never felt so out of control. His entire career had been built on adhering to rigid rules, whether military or his own. Now he couldn't seem to find a valid reason for either.

But he had to. He had to end this now.

He didn't move.

A slow smile toyed with the corners of her mouth, a game-changer smile, and he knew he'd given too much away. With a deep breath she crossed the room and locked the door, ironically one of the few things in this place still to work. Then, swinging back to face him, she advanced, hesitantly at first.

And then she was standing in front of him, her breathing as ragged and shallow as his felt. They stood, motionless, watching each other for the longest time. Finally, she lifted her hand and placed it on his chest, over his heart. He felt a droplet of emotion swelling inside, and it plinked onto the frozen glacier of his heart. But he knew only too well that the icy block was so big, so compact it would take a river of warm water and more years than he had on this earth to melt it.

And, still, a part of him actually longed to let her try. To see if Elle could be the one person to help him heal the pain of how he'd let his mother and sister die. How he'd let Janine think he didn't care about her, or about their unborn baby before it, too, had been lost. He was selfish, just like his father. He *had* to push Elle away, for her own protection.

He grasped at the only life raft he could see.

'Careful, Major.'

She stopped, blinked. Then shook it off.

'Oh, no, Fitz, that's not fair.' She almost managed to disguise the quiver in her tone, but he was attuned to her. 'You don't get to pick and choose when to follow the rules here. I was ready to show you to your office and walk away, to leave things on a professional footing, on a military footing. But *you* ordered me to come in and *you* made things personal when you brought up our intimate past. You made this about Elle and Fitz, woman and man, not Major and Colonel. So right now you don't get to pull rank like that. If you don't want this then you tell me to stop as Elle. Don't use excuses.'

The air practically crackled around them, tension twisting his insides as the blood pumped around his body. She was unmistakeably determined to stand her ground. So it turned out that life raft was actually an old naval mine.

She was no closer and yet he felt she was all around him. She was all he could see, all he could hear, all he could smell. The more he resisted, the softer she seemed to make her tone. Not harsh, or in his face, but the most feminine of challenges tumbled out of her tempting lips. She didn't have to say the words. He knew it was on him. He could turn around and walk away.

But he didn't. She was so close he could almost taste her.

'Even if I kiss you, it won't change anything.'

'So you say.'

She lifted her other hand. Both palms were flat on his chest and he felt another rush of intoxicating need.

He dipped his head, stopping millimetres before making contact. So close her breath rippled along his cheek.

She tilted her head up a fraction further, angling it perfectly without making contract. A silent power play, but instead of claiming it for themselves they were each offering it to the other.

'Last chance,' she whispered.

He had to push her away now.

Instead, he sneaked one hand around her waist, hauling her to him. Then he dipped his head and claimed her mouth with his, revelling in the sensations that cascaded over him at her touch, her feel, her taste. As if he'd been stranded in the barren wasteland outside for far, far too long, and she was his oasis.

She tasted every bit as heady as he recalled, her body fitting to his like she was made for him, her teeth grazing his bottom lip with the lightest of touches, her soft sighs sending his willpower scattering.

With a low groan, Fitz angled his head, deepening her kiss to something much more urgent and demanding, revelling in the way her lips parted for him, and the soft sound that came from somewhere in the back of her throat. He forgot that he was meant to be warning her to safeguard herself. He forgot that he would inevitably hurt her as his father had hurt those around him.

He forgot everything. He simply indulged. For what seemed like an eternity, his mouth slid over hers. When he pushed, she pushed back. When he held back, Elle sought him. He trailed kisses down her jaw, her collarbone and to the hollow at the base of her neck. Her shivers of pleasure stoked his need. And each time he returned to those plump, pink lips, her mouth reached for his and her tongue met his in the same sinfully sinuous dance.

As he gave himself up to the sensations, as each kiss from Elle threatened to undermine every defence he'd spent years putting in place, the plink of those warm droplets on his ice-block heart grew more insistent.

Before he could help himself, he'd released the curtain of reds and golds from its military bun, inhaling its familiar fresh, floral scent as his hands buried themselves in its luxuriant depths. He could recall exactly how it had felt brushing over his naked skin that night and his body tightened.

She felt it instantly; he could feel the sweet uplift of her smile against his lips, and then she rocked against him.

'Gabriella,' he groaned, unable to make up his mind whether it was a groan or a warning growl.

And still he kissed her, sometimes gently and reverently, other times hard and greedily. As though he never wanted to stop. He didn't know when he backed her up so that she was sitting on his desk with him standing between her legs, or when his fingers crept under the hem of her tee, or when he lifted it over her head and dropped it in a puddle on the plans he was supposed to be going through.

He just knew his hands were sweeping over velvet skin he'd been dreaming about for a week, running over her ribs and circling her body so that his thumbs were grazing the lower swell of her perfect breasts.

He needed to stop. Needed to remind her—remind himself—what kind of a man he was. How he would inevitably hurt her.

'So, what now?' he managed harshly, shocked by the sheer force of his own driving desire. 'We give in to this thing between us? Here, now? Tell me, Elle, do you want it on the uneven floor or on the rusty metal desk?'

Any other woman would have fled, intimidated by the tone, let alone the words. Elle merely sparkled brighter, as though she enjoyed the push-pull of it. He couldn't work it out.

'So this is what the real Fitz looks like,' she murmured, moving her hands down his body. Though he could hear the quiver in her voice. 'Not quite as cool and utterly in control as everyone might think. I like this side of you, the side behind the mask.'

'Elle…'

'I want what you want. One more night.'

It wasn't encouraged or condoned by the army, but they both knew it happened. As long as they were utterly discreet, and, like Elle had pointed out before, they were both commissioned officers and he wasn't her boss.

He glanced at the desk. It wasn't his style. It wasn't her style. But he knew that in that instant they both wanted each other too much to care.

He *had* to put the brakes on it.

It felt as though it took every last bit of strength in his body to move his hands to her upper arms and push her away.

'I can't let this happen.' His voice actually cracked.

'I take responsibility for myself, Fitz,' she told him, her eyes glittering with desire so hot it scorched him.

'It isn't that simple.'

Raw need pulsed between them but he couldn't give in to it.

'I think it is. Why do you have such rigid rules for yourself?' she asked, the soft voice piercing through the heart of his fears better than any arrow could. 'Who are you trying to protect yourself from?'

'I'm trying to protect you.' He gritted his teeth so hard he was surprised his jaw didn't crack.

'From whom? You?' She shook her head. 'Why?'

He didn't want to answer. He'd never volunteered his story to anyone before. And yet under her coaxing the words spilled from his lips and there was nothing he could do to stop them.

'That car crash with my mother and sister was my fault.'

'I didn't think you were there.' She squinted up at him.

'Exactly. I wasn't there, but I should have been. I was too busy enjoying myself on a night out with friends. We were celebrating a week early. My mum had been a barmaid at the local pub for a few years; they treated her a bit like a manager and every time someone didn't turn up for a shift they'd call her and she'd rush over there to fill in.'

Even now he could remember just how aggrieved he'd felt, as though she was deliberately ruining their precious family time together when all she'd been doing had been trying to keep her job so the meagre income would keep the roof over their heads and some food on the table. All he'd ever thought was that it was never enough. He shook off the memories, forcing himself to carry on, to show Elle exactly what kind of man he was.

'I sometimes felt they didn't employ enough

staff just because they knew they could turn to her and she'd cover it all. So from the age of about fifteen I became the babysitter. Nights out with schoolfriends were inevitably cancelled because she'd get called in and I'd end up looking after my baby sister. And I began to resent it.'

'So that night you went out?' Elle asked quietly. 'How could you have known any different?'

'Because she phoned me. Fifteen messages, each one more frantic than the last. She called me to tell me my father had found us, that he was drunk and that she'd hidden my sister in the cup-board over the stairs.'

'Fitz…'

He ignored her, determined to carry on. Fight-ing the overwhelming guilt and regret.

'I saw the missed calls and I turned my phone off. By the time I listened to the calls it was hours later. I raced home but of course I was far too late.'

'Fitz,' she gasped. 'That must have been… I can't imagine how that must have been. But you can't honestly blame yourself. How could you have known? You were seventeen, a kid, you couldn't have foreseen your father had found you.'

'I should have cared enough to listen. I should

have taken her call, not shut it down as though she didn't deserve my time.'

'That's ridiculous,' Elle cried, but he ignored the emotions her words threatened to stir in him.

He didn't know why she insisted on seeing him in such a bold, fair light, but she had it wrong.

'You don't understand. I let them down. I wasn't there for them when they needed me. I was thoughtless, selfish, I was just like *him*.'

He practically spat the last word out in disgust, and still Elle looked at him with empathy, and care, as though she understood. As though he wasn't the self-serving young man he'd actually been. But he knew the truth. He knew he could have been there for them. He *should* have been there for them.

Just like with Janine. He should have been there for her and then she would never have lost her baby.

Their baby.

He'd tried to make himself love her. He'd told himself that if he could love her, maybe he wasn't as broken as he'd feared. But he couldn't. Janine was sweet and kind, and she'd loved him. But he'd been unable to feel the same about her. He hadn't been capable of it. He'd ended up using her. She'd been right, she'd have been better off never meeting him.

Just as Elle would be.

He opened his mouth to tell her, then stopped. What if she told him it wouldn't have made a difference? For any of them? He might actually allow himself to believe her. She was so understanding, so empathetic, so damned convincing. She looked at him as though he was a good man and he wanted so much to be the human being she saw.

He was a good leader, a good soldier. But he wasn't a good man.

Another plink and he could swear he felt the tiniest fissure race through the block of ice that surrounded his heart.

It suddenly occurred to him that if she melted it then he would have to feel again.

All that pain he'd stuffed down for so long.

Fear finally galvanised him and he found his voice, as raw and biting as it sounded.

'You don't see it, do you, Elle? It was sex. That's all it was.'

He told himself he didn't regret the flash of hurt his harshness caused in Elle's eyes. That, in the long run, this was the only way to protect her from him. But he knew he was hurting her. He knew the rejection burned her more than anything after the way her ex had already rejected her, betrayed her.

So what kind of a man was he, to play on an insecurity he knew ate away at her? And still he couldn't stop.

'I'm not the man you want me to be.' He rammed the point home before he could change his mind. 'That person is a figment of your imagination.'

'You're lying,' she whispered.

Hopeful.

Pleading.

More than anything he wanted to tell her she was right. She knew him better than she realised. Better than anyone else ever had.

Instead he told himself it was for the best. That whatever hurt she was feeling now was nothing compared to the misery he would inevitably cause her if they let anything happen between them. If he let her down, too.

So he steeled his resolve and kept heading for the door. She'd been right in the first place when she'd wanted to avoid this discussion, but he was the one who had insisted on it.

Why? Because he really had wanted to create

a clear division between that night and now? Or because deep down there was a part of him that didn't want to let her slip through his fingers a second time?

As if she'd ever been his to lose.

'I don't have time for nonsense like this. I have a briefing to get to,' he threw over his shoulder, refusing to look back.

Because to do so would mean looking at Elle and if he saw her he wouldn't be able to walk out that door; he'd go straight back to her, take her in his arms and surrender to her instead.

But capitulation wasn't an option. If he didn't end it now, he feared he might end up telling her things he'd never told anyone else. Ever. He might let her into that dark corner of his soul in the hope that her brilliant light might finally make it feel less black. It would open too many old wounds.

And that would only end up laying waste to both of them.

CHAPTER NINE

'YOU SEE THE ulcer lies on the antrum of the patient's stomach?' Elle glanced at her student. 'So what would you suggest?'

'Wedge excision,' Amir said confidently. 'Closure of the consequential defect should be achieved fairly easily without significant deformation of the stomach.'

'Good.' Elle nodded. 'And if the ulcer had instead been along the lesser curvature of the stomach?'

'It would be more problematic. More prone to re-bleeding because of the rich complex of blood vessels from the left gastric artery.'

'Anything else?'

Amir paused, and she couldn't be sure whether it was the language barrier or a gap in his knowledge. Many of the local doctors here were on an extremely steep learning curve but she was continually impressed by their eagerness to soak up everything she and her team were teaching them.

And having a CO like Phil, who didn't just have decades of experience as a brilliant surgeon but was also an inspiring teacher, certainly kept Elle at her best. It was a challenge she usually relished.

But not today.

For the past couple of days all she'd wanted to do was stay in her army cot, lick her wounds, and hope that everything looked a little less grim when Fitz finally left the hospital camp and headed back to Razorwire.

That, obviously, hadn't been an option. But at least she'd managed to avoid him since that awful day in his office, to give herself the chance to start thinking straight again. At first she'd vacillated between rage and mortification. Rage that he'd lifted the lid on their attraction and mortification that he'd shut her down so completely.

She dragged her mind back to the present and to Amir.

'Okay, wedge excision of gastric ulcers along the lesser curvature of the stomach is harder to do and is much more likely to result in a deformed J-shaped stomach and luminal obstruction or gastric volvulus, which is rotation of the stomach by more than one hundred and eighty degrees...'

'Yes, yes.' Amir nodded vigorously. 'Inconstant blood loss, obstruction of materials moving through the stomach, and sometimes tissue death.'

'Okay, good.' Elle smiled. 'We'll go over it again, it's something you're likely to come across often here. Right, let's see what we can do for our patient here.'

She worked carefully, talking Amir through each step, until finally she was satisfied, taking half a step back and straightening her spine.

'Did you ask your Colonel Duggan if you can continue here, or return on…what you call it, a *back-to-back* tour when this tour of yours now is over?'

Lifting her head, Elle glanced into the hopeful expression on Amir's face. Having started this tour of duty at Razorwire, once her three months here were up, two more rotations of army doctors would take over during the course of the next twelve months, and Elle had hoped to be able to return on the last one. The fact that Amir also hoped she would return spoke volumes about her teaching style and Elle couldn't help smiling proudly.

'Colonel Duggan, yes. I did chat with him while he was here, unofficially of course. He considered the possibility of me returning within the year was quite high, but there's no guarantee, of course.'

'That's wonderful news. You are so dedicated to your career, you sacrifice greatly to be a soldier doctor, yes? But it is your life, you are single-minded, and you are not needing anything else. It inspires much.'

'Thank you,' Elle managed graciously, trying not to frown. 'Right, you recall the suture technique I demonstrated yesterday? Good. Because I want you to close up now.'

Amir nodded, clearly pleased, and stepped forward, leaving Elle, her eyes still on the surgery, to wonder if she wasn't a little too single-minded.

How else to forge a career like this? Fitz must have done the same. Was that what he'd meant about not being good for her? She could hardly square the Fitz she'd met that night with the Colonel who was out here. It wasn't so much like two sides to the one man as it was two completely different men. The man from that night who had told her things about his past, about his family, had been very different from the man who had stood in front of her the other day and lied to her. She was sure of it.

Clearly Major Howes knew Fitz well from the past and still liked and respected him, and, from what little she could tell, so did the rest of the men in the troop from Fitz's regiment. And surely they should know—he was *their* commanding officer after all. He might only just be at the start of his two-year posting as their colonel but morale among them had certainly appeared boosted in the few days he'd been on site.

She couldn't shake the idea that none of them had ever seen the Fitz *she'd* met that night. Neither could she shake the idea that there had been more between them that night than either of them had realised. Enough for him to tell her things he'd never told anyone. And after the way Stevie had lied to her, she valued honesty more than ever.

Either way it was irrelevant. She shook the thought away irritably. She was never going to get the chance to find out. Fitz had made it more than clear that as much as he was still attracted to her, he wasn't interested in opening himself up to anyone. As for her, she'd obviously let herself get too emotionally involved to be any good at no-strings sex. And the wounds from her years with Stevie were still too fresh, she wasn't ready for another relationship. Not that it was even on the cards with Fitz.

So where did that leave her?

With your career, she reminded herself firmly. When all else failed, she'd always have her role as an army doctor to rely on. She drowned out the little voice that suggested that she might have liked to have known Fitz just a little better. As he'd said, he wasn't the man she'd imagined him to be.

She shrugged off her gloomy thoughts and leaned in to check Amir's sutures.

She might have nothing back home, but she had her career and hadn't that always been the most important thing to her? And right now she had command of a hospital that, partially destroyed or not, brought different cases every day.

While Royal Engineers and logistics units worked on building, rebuilding and refitting the old hospital so that some of the major international charities would send teams out over the coming years, her job was to keep the medical side running in the meantime. Local communities were desperate to be able to use the hospital again, instead of having to make the hazardous four-hour drive across the border to the next closest hospital. No one wanted to risk the drive if they could avoid it, with the unsafe roads and dangerous checkpoint crossing, not to mention the fact that, out here, it was down to the men to allow their wives or children to seek medical help, so the more accessible it was, the easier that would be.

But with so few surgeons and doctors there was no place for specialties and the experience was testing and refreshing her knowledge all the time. Elle found it both exciting and challenging, with patients ranging from babies to the elderly, and from victims who'd stepped on old, forgotten landmines to women having labour problems. In fact, the latter accounted for a huge percentage of her operations, given maternal mortality was so high out here, all of which was a far cry from the combat trauma she'd been doing in other postings over the last few years. She couldn't afford to let Fitz ruin what was otherwise a unique career opportunity for her.

What had Fitz said? That he destroyed everything? That he'd destroy her?

She was beginning to understand just how close to the mark that was.

Shaking the bleak thoughts from her head, Elle concentrated on her task of watching her student work, commenting if necessary but trying to take a step back as much as she could. Amir's work was neat and clean; he picked things up quickly but he also listened well and watched closely. He would likely be a real asset to the hospital in very little time, which was good since he'd have his work cut out for him.

Finally, he was closing up on the perforated ulcer patient.

'Nice job,' she congratulated him. 'How would you feel about heading up a mobile team on your own this time? We're due to carry out a round of measles and polio vaccinations for infants in some of the outlying communities.'

A surprised look crossed the young doctor's face, swiftly replaced by a proud one.

'I'd like that very much.'

'I'm not sure but I heard something about a sandstorm being due in the next couple of days,' one of the voluntary aid nurses interjected apologetically. 'Of course you can never be sure, and there's every chance you might get out and back before it even hits, but…'

'But you can't be too safe.' Elle flashed her a bright smile to reassure her. 'Then we'll hold back for now but pick your team and as soon as we get the all-clear you can go, Amir.'

'Thank you,' he nodded. 'I will.'

'Major?'

Elle craned her neck around as one of the designated liaison soldiers stood at the edge of the privacy screen, evidently having heard the exchange and concluding he wouldn't be disturbing them. He could have been there for any length of time, waiting patiently while they carried out the operation.

For the moment, the simple screen set-up was the only thing to separate the delivery room from the open ward. In a few months it would all look completely different and would be significantly more sterile and high-tech. For now, it was all they had.

'What is it, Corporal?' With a final check on Amir's work, Elle stepped around the screen.

'Colonel Fitzwilliam asked if you were available to go through a couple of design modifications with him and Major Howes for the power and water supplies to the hospital.'

And just like that, her heart slammed against her chest wall. He'd had the presence to include Major Howes in the message but she couldn't work out whether it was a good thing or a bad one. They would have a buffer, true, but there would be even more pressure to act normally—whatever that meant—around Fitz, and she wasn't sure she was enough of an actress to pull it off.

'We're almost done here.' Elle had no idea how

the words came out, as strangled as they sounded to her ears.

The corporal, however, didn't seem to notice anything amiss.

'Ma'am.'

'Will you inform the Colonel I'll be there within the half-hour?'

'Yes, Major.'

She watched him leave and stood motionless long after the double doors had closed and stilled behind the lad. Her hands felt sticky, her heart was racing, and none of it was due to the searing temperatures inside that operating area. She'd performed two Caesareans and overseen the perforated ulcer operation pretty much back to back this morning, and yet one mention of Fitz and she was instantly flustered. It didn't bode well for their future working relationship.

Finally, almost jerkily, she managed to get her legs moving again and rounded the screen to help Amir finish up. The last suture was put in place as a strange rattling began and the ground felt like it was shaking beneath their feet.

Earthquake. Not uncommon out here and probably some distance away, but it was certainly a strong one. She grabbed hold of the bed, more concerned that the patient didn't fall to the floor.

It seemed as though the very earth was mirroring her uncertainty out here. She snorted quietly to herself and waited for the quake to end.

'So the Colonel and I thought we could extend this part of the facility...' Carl tapped the plans with the tip of his pencil '...and move the ICU to where the ORs would have been, and therefore demolish the block where the ICU is currently planned to be.'

'That won't work.' Elle shook her head, keeping her focus firmly on Carl, as she had during the entire briefing.

If she allowed herself to look at Fitz, even once, she was afraid she would crumple, but now she could see him in her peripheral vision, moving forward in his chair.

'Why not, Major?' he demanded tightly.

She bristled. That steely part of her core that had been AWOL for the last few days started to hum back into life. She composed herself and faced him.

'The ICU would still connect to the ORs, Colonel,' she acknowledged, 'but that's a long way around for one of the wards. In an emergency it would take too long and I'd end up having to rush men to Theatre through the women's ward, or vice versa.'

'Ah, I see.' She could almost hear his tone relax. *Had he been as apprehensive about this meeting as her?*

Somehow, that made her feel a fraction better.

'Then there's another option.' Fitz moved his hand across the plans and she shivered, stopping herself from recalling quite how that strong palm had felt on her skin. 'If we moved the ORs to this location we could put the plant room for the medical gas supply system here. The ICU would go here and the wards could be there, or there. The generators would then go here and we could even tap into the aquifer with a new pipeline to ensure the running water for the facility is as clean as it possibly can be until the government builds a new waste management plant next year.'

Quickly, she ran it over and over in her head. It looked promising, although her sixth sense told her there was one area that could be improved from a medical point of view, but which they couldn't have foreseen as engineers.

'Would that work for you, Major?' Fitz asked.

'It looks like a viable solution and I like the sound of it,' she mused. 'I might like to make a couple of tweaks to the internal layout designs if it's to work optimally. How long do I have to go over it?'

'How long do you need?'

Fitz's voice was so flat she couldn't work out what he was thinking.

'Not long. I'd like to get it back to you by the end of today, as long as we don't get an influx of emergencies. With Colonel Duggan back at Razorwire, we're down a surgeon and a teacher.'

'At the moment we're still going through the hospital itself to make the last structural repairs to the east wing, such as it is.' Carl smiled. 'But I'd like to start on the external foundations this week. I'm heading out with a logistics convoy to inspect the ongoing railhead operation in the north and won't be back until tomorrow, so what if I leave the plans with you overnight and then go through them with you when I return?'

Her body numbed.

If Carl was going off-site then it meant that if there were any issues needing immediate discussion or resolution she'd have to deal with Fitz directly. The thought of having to work on anything *one on one* with him set her stomach churning with fear.

'I'm heading a medical convoy out into the communities myself tomorrow.' She sent out a silent apology to Amir for taking his place after she'd just offered it to him. 'I'll be gone for a few days.' She feigned apology. 'I could look at it tonight and then pass it to my second-in-command to go through it with you?'

Fitz spoke before Carl could answer.

'Major Howes, if you could ask Staff Sergeant Bell to start on that area of ground we discussed this morning?'

'Colonel.' Carl dipped his head, heading quickly out of the door.

Fitz waited for it to close before confronting her.

'Why are you taking a mobile medical unit into the communities?'

Elle raised her eyebrow. They both knew the question wasn't within his remit as commanding officer of the Royal Engineers. She could have challenged him, but instead she chose to play it straight down the line as strictly professional.

'I have a wave of IPVs to administer.'

'IPVs?'

'Inactivated polio vaccines. Part of the medical role out here is to ensure every child under the age of ten has been vaccinated against polio and measles. We can't guarantee the husbands will make the trip to me for their children so until the charities arrive to begin the grandmothers' health groups, we stand more chance of getting the men to agree if we go to them.'

'And the grandmothers' health groups are...?'

'Like many of the places the charities have worked, out here it's down to the men to decide whether their wives and children can get medical help. Over the decades they've found that the most effective way to encourage attitude change is to teach the grandmothers. They are some of the most valued and respected people within their communities and they have more influence over their sons and sons-in-law than the young wives do over their husbands.'

'I see. But until we've completed a lot of the rebuild, the charities aren't going to be out here. So going into the communities makes them more amenable?'

'Sure. A lot of it is more about lack of information and advice than anything. Not all families have the means, or inclination, to get to the hospital, so I go to them. We try to educate them on why getting their child immunised is so important, and describe symptoms such as acute flaccid paralysis so that they know what to look out for and when to bring their child to us at the hospital.'

'Which communities?' he bit out.

'Say again?'

'When you head out tomorrow, which direction?'

'South-west.' She frowned. 'I don't see—'

'Is that entirely necessary? The region isn't safe at the moment,' Fitz cut her off, oblivious. 'There are severe dust storms in that area at the moment, advancing walls of dust and debris that can be miles wide and thousands of feet high.'

'Yes, thank you.' She bit her tongue from giving a flippant retort and battled to keep her voice even. 'This isn't my first tour of duty, I *have* come across dust storms before.'

For a moment she thought she saw a flash of concern on Fitz's face. Then it was gone.

'Good, then I shouldn't need to tell you that heading into the local communities right now is a bad idea. There are wide expanses in that direction, the roads are barely roads and the risk of RTAs is much higher.'

Her irritation, her discomfort all dissolved as a wisp of empathy curled its way up from her stomach. She recalled that haunted look in his eyes from the first night, pained and helpless, when he'd told her how his family had died in a crash. His father, drink-driving. A murmur escaped her lips.

'This is about the crash, isn't it? You're worried about a convoy crash?'

There were units driving in and out of the site all the time, especially logistics convoys as they ferried supplies. So, perhaps more accurately, he was worried about *her* convoy being caught by a rapidly moving wall of dust.

She was absurdly touched, even as his face turned deathly white. Abruptly his eyes burned with fury, searing her to the spot, a snarl twisting the features she'd touched, kissed, tasted.

'Why would you say that?' he rasped, his anger bouncing off the walls, making the tiny room throb.

Anyone else might be intimidated. Elle refused to allow herself to be. Instead, she peered at him.

'You don't remember telling me about your mum and sister?'

'I remember,' he ground out, as if waiting for her to say something else.

She licked her lips, steadying herself.

'I think you feel somehow responsible. Maybe for not being there. Maybe because they died and you lived. But because you couldn't control that situation, you're concerned about my convoy going out tomorrow.'

The silence swelled and the small space felt even more stifled, like a pressurised can left out in the sweltering sun. But she wasn't about to back down.

'That's it?' His bark of laughter rang out, a hollow and unpleasant sound.

'Isn't it enough?' she asked softly.

And then, oddly, she could have sworn *relief* flickered in those eyes, swiftly chased by disdain.

'I suppose it is.' He shrugged. 'But, no, telling you about my family was a combination of factors from that night; let me assure you it wasn't anything special about *you*. I was merely concerned about your team in Colonel Duggan's absence. So, if you've quite finished psychoanalysing me...'

It was all she could do to stay upright. His words were as cutting as if he'd taken her out by the knee, winding her and humiliating her in one smooth strike. *What a fool she was for thinking he'd been worried about her.* When was she going to get it through her head that whatever they'd shared that night, in Fitz's head it was over and done with?

CHAPTER TEN

HE REGRETTED THE words as soon as they'd left his lips but that did little to reduce their efficacy. His low blow had clearly left her reeling and he hated himself for it.

He was supposed to be protecting Elle from himself by keeping her at arm's length so that he wouldn't destroy her. He wasn't supposed to be destroying her in the process.

'I'm sorry. That was…uncalled for,' he told her quietly, sincerely.

She inclined her head stiffly, plainly struggling to compose herself.

'I appreciate your concern for my convoy, Colonel, but it's misplaced. Furthermore, I would respectfully remind you that Colonel Duggan and I are running the medical side of this mission and I have administrative and operational command in his absence. I'm satisfied that the risk of dust storms is no greater than usual in this area. If we get caught out, as convoys frequently do around here, we'll follow protocol and find shelter or at least pull off the road to wait it out.'

So stiff, so formal. He'd really hurt her.

'I did try to warn you, even from that first night, that I wasn't a good man. That I always end up destroying people.'

She pressed her lips together, her back bracing just a fraction.

'I'm sure I don't have to tell you that dust storms in this area are unpredictable, Colonel, so we're going to have to take a chance at some point. And, to refer to your earlier question, yes, it *is* necessary,' she cut in respectfully but firmly. 'There are refugees crossing the border in their hundreds of thousands, and even though there are vaccination stations at many of the crossings there are still tens of thousands, if not hundreds of thousands, of children and babies who are missing out and who have already moved on and into existing communities. If I can spare children from suffering polio paralysis then I have to go, possible sandstorm or not.'

He almost smiled as her voice changed when she spoke of her work. That passion of hers had been one of the things to attract him in the first place. And the fact that she was desperately clinging to formality and keeping the topic mission-related hadn't gone unnoticed either. Normally, he wouldn't have pushed it—then again, normally he wouldn't have been in this position to start with—but that…tenderness she'd demonstrated moments ago when she'd spoken of his family, of his loss, told him that she'd been touched at the idea he'd been worried for her safety.

He owed her the truth.

'I'm sorry, Elle, but I tried to warn you I wasn't a good man, whatever you might think of me right now.'

Her shoulders actually sagged.

A strange silence descended over them and he had to let her be the one to break it. But when she did, he wasn't prepared for the sadness in her voice as it tore into his chest.

'I never thought you were cruel, Fitz, even without seeing the way your men love and respect you. But you can't keep doing this, flip-flopping between acknowledging this attraction between us one minute and then pushing me away the next.'

'I'm just trying to do the right thing.' He shook his head.

'You create barriers,' she countered. 'You never intended to tell me those secrets of yours that first night, but you decided it didn't matter because we were never going to see each other again; even if I hadn't been set on one crazy night, *you* would have made sure of it. And then when we turned up here together you resented me for it. You've been using army barriers, rules that don't technically exist, to push me away ever since.'

How did she do it? How did she see that side of him that no one else had, and yet fail to see the swirling darkness within him?

'Why do you want to be with me?' he demanded hotly, standing abruptly and rounding the desk so there was nothing between them. 'I'm not a good man. I'm not the responsible, caring man you seem to think I am.'

'Tell that to those men out there who think the world of you!' she exclaimed.

They were so close he could feel her body heat, experience the emotion as it poured off her, her fierceness making his chest ache. Yet, deliberately, neither of them closed the gap any further.

'Tell that to the men they've spoken to back home and at Razorwire who spoke so highly of you, leading from the front in more combat zones than they could remember. Tell that to High Command, who appointed you as one of the youngest lieutenant colonels.'

He wanted to believe her. So much that it hurt. He couldn't.

'That's just the army. I like the man I am when I'm serving. The responsibility, the care, the life is different. It's easy to be a good leader, I know what's expected of me.'

'No, it's easy because it's who you are.' She heaved out a shaky sigh.

He bowed his head towards hers.

'But that's not the man I am out *there*, away from the structure. Where real feelings are needed. I don't have them. I'm empty, and broken, and toxic.'

Much closer and their heads would have touched. That last absence of contact was the only thing saving either of them right now.

'I don't believe that,' she whispered at length. 'Because that's not the man I met that night. *Just Fitz* opened up to me because he wanted to. A thoughtful, considerate, sensitive man in the bar with that young lad, and then later with me, in bed. I couldn't have hoped for anyone more giving or generous to make me feel respected. You made me feel desirable again.'

'You wouldn't say that if you knew the things I've done. The lives I've destroyed. I can't forget my mistakes, I can't pretend they were okay.'

'Everybody makes mistakes, Fitz. The trick is to learn from them.'

'Why don't you have the sense to walk away?' He demanded. 'I *have* learned from my mistakes. I learned that I'm just like my old man. Selfish, joyless, destructive.'

'Funny,' she whispered, 'but that isn't a description I recognise, and neither would your old friend Major Howes, who speaks of you so highly.'

'That's because I'm a different person here.'

'Then let me say that it isn't the side of you that I saw that night.'

Pain expanded in his chest, almost crushing everything else.

'But it would be. If that night was allowed to be something more.' His voice sounded raw even to his ears. 'That's why I'm trying to shield you.'

Her whisper was so low he had to strain to hear her.

'See, that's where I have the difficulty. If you're so much this selfish person, then why would you be trying to shield me?'

He stiffened, momentarily thrown. She made

him *want* to believe in himself the way she seemed to.

'Because there's worse you don't know about.'

'So, try me.'

Hot. Urgent. Desperate.

And he wanted to. He wanted to tell her everything, to lay every last, ugly truth out there and let her smooth it away, the way he suspected she could.

But if she didn't, if she saw what he'd been trying to hide all along, the mirror image of his father, Fitz didn't think he could bear it.

It was a reminder he needed.

This wasn't about him. This was about Elle. If they hadn't ended up here, at this hospital, in this place, they would never have tried to see each other again. He ignored the voice that reminded him how he'd been considering contacting the hotel about her when he came back off his tour of duty, however unlikely it was they might have assisted. And, yes, it was more than just sex, it felt like there was some kind of connection there. But how long would that last? It would disappear in the end. He'd feel stifled, trapped, just as he had with Janine. And then, despite his best intentions, hurting Elle would be inevitable.

'I have to live with the consequences of my choices every day,' he bit out, firmer now. 'But I *can* make sure I don't hurt a single other person. I *can* make sure I don't destroy you.'

It was for the best.

'Except that you can't, can you?' Elle whispered. 'You keep trying to push me away but then you can't help yourself, you have to reel me back in. You might not mean to but you do. You obviously care about me in some small way when you worry about a dust storm, but when I challenge you, you call me a meaningless fling. How is that not hurting me?'

He froze. As much as he might not want to admit it, there was merit to her words. From the moment they'd met he'd felt some kind of connection with her and he'd found it next to impossible to leave her the next day without also leaving his phone number, even though he'd come to his senses and binned it.

He'd dragged her into his office and dredged it all up that first day he'd turned up to see her, and he'd allowed himself to kiss her, to convey all the confusion neither of them could articulate. And now he'd dragged her here again, dismissed Carl, engineered things to be with her. He should have left days ago. He could have worked on the plans back at Razorwire, but this was where Elle was.

The more he pushed her away, the more aware he seemed to be of her. As though the fact that she was out here on site, yet avoiding him, left him feeling illogically hollow. The more she avoided him, the more she took up residence in his head. Instead of her absence helping to quell his ache for her, it only made him want her all the more. *Crave her.*

And not just physically. He ached to hear her laugh, see her smile, feel the warm glow that accompanied her presence.

Just because she was out of sight it didn't mean he hadn't gathered as much information as he could about her from the other officers around the site, both those who had worked with her for years and those who had just started to get to know her on this mission.

Yet the answers were always the same. She was respected, admired, liked and not infrequently lusted after, though no one but Carl openly admitted it. As a man who was suffering from the same affliction he could recognise the signs, not least because it caused a fresh sense of possession to course through his veins.

He could hear a muffled part of his brain proposing that if pushing her away and distancing himself from Elle wasn't working, then perhaps allowing himself to spend time with her, saturating himself with her presence would do the job. More time with her would allow him to see her as just another woman, flawed like everyone else. He could stop elevating her, could stop seeing her through the sentimental eyes of that first night, when the grim anniversary of his family's deaths had already been stirring long-buried emotions inside him, and which Elle had inadvertently tapped into.

The events of that night had created a false sense of connection with her, and that was what was causing him to lose his head now. It was stopping him from focussing on a job to which he'd never had any issue applying himself in the past.

If he allowed himself to explore being with Elle, then perhaps he would finally be able to shake off this unreasonably acute, distracting need to know her, to understand her.

And if they both knew the rules of any such encounter from the outset, if they both agreed it was temporary, an extension of that one night, then surely he could also set aside his fear that he would hurt her. He'd never worried about that with previous relationships, he'd never let that stop him.

But Elle wasn't like them. She was different. *He* felt different with her.

He needed time to think.

'I'm trying to protect you,' Fitz eventually stated flatly. 'That's the last thing I'm going to say. For now.'

He didn't know how he did it, but he finally tore himself away from her and moved back around the desk.

'When do you leave?' he asked.

The hurt that made her whole body slump almost wrecked him.

'Elle, I'm asking as Fitz. Not as a colonel. I'm not using protocol as an excuse. I know what you said last time.'

It was the only concession he could make to her, and he was relieved when she nodded, dredging up a faint smile, acknowledging it for what it was. He wasn't shutting her down like he had last time. He was buying himself time. And she was prepared to sell it to him.

'We leave at dawn. It's a couple of hours' drive

so we'll get most of tomorrow and then all of the following day. We'll head back the day after.'

'Okay.' He nodded.

So tomorrow he'd either be heading back to Razorwire, putting Elle into his past for good, or staying here and riding this attraction out until he could finally let her go.

He barely had the night to decide.

'He can't be serious?'

Fitz could hear Elle's muttered objection as she stood alone, her back to him, in the deserted square outside the hospital, the sunrise giving an almost halo effect to her flame-red hair. She was far enough from the hospital that she couldn't be heard, but close enough that she could watch the convoy go through its final preparations without standing out against the backdrop of the building.

'Something amiss?' he asked casually as he walked up behind her, and she spun around with a startled cry.

She eyed him cautiously, as though recognising his less controlled, less distant attitude but still uncertain what it meant.

'There's a three-vehicle engineers' convoy alongside my medical one, Colonel,' she said, as she indicated towards where the vehicles were parked, less than a couple of hundred metres away, one of which was a four-by-four towing a boring rig.

'Indeed there is,' he agreed brightly.

Was it wrong that it gave him such a perverse pleasure to beat her at her own game?

She narrowed her eyes a fraction.

'May I ask to what purpose, sir?'

'You may. Although given that there's no one immediately around I think we can dispense with the formality at this time, don't you?' he countered lightly. 'Anyway, I realised that accompanying the mobile medical unit into the local communities could be advantageous to my men. As part of our mission in this area, the Royal Engineers are to be responsible for digging new wells and building schools throughout various communities in the region. After all the conflict over the last few decades, the people here are naturally suspicious of non-locals but they *do* accept the medical units.'

'So you want to accompany us to trade off our good reputation?' she asked slowly.

He grinned, knowing she couldn't fault his logic.

'And gain their trust more easily in order to perform a couple of test drills at each site you visit, yes. Furthermore, padding out your convoy will make you less of a target and mean only one lot of force protection will be required.'

Not that anyone was particularly expecting trouble in a non-combat area but a security detail was more about appearances.

'I see. So...?' she started, then paused, concluding feebly with another, 'I see.'

She still thought it was about his fears over the safety of her convoy after his mother's car crash. She wasn't entirely off the mark, though it wasn't the car crash that haunted him when he thought of Elle. The idea of her being out there, risking some of the most severe dust storms the region had experienced in a decade, brought fear and old demons to assail him. He knew all too well the impact of one of these dust storms on a military convoy. And he was fairly certain that Elle was only heading up that convoy as an excuse to get away from site, from him, for a couple of days. After the way he'd treated her, he could understand it.

If anything happened to Elle the way it had to Janine...all because of him...

'I just... I don't know if we have time,' Elle

hazarded. 'Setting up your rig and doing your test drills will take time. We were intending to make this a brief dash. Get out there, vaccinate, head back.'

'Indeed? Only yesterday you gave the impression you might be out there for a couple of days.'

She flushed.

'You know these things are never straightforward.'

'And you appear to have a vehicle loaded up with hens sent by one of the charities.' He quashed a smile. 'Presumably this is part of the nutrition and economic sustainability initiative? Give each family a couple of hens so that they have free eggs and, as they gain experience, the surplus can be sold at market to give them money to buy other supplies. All of which will take time.'

The corners of her mouth tightened with guilt. 'Yes…well…'

He didn't blame her for pushing him away. He wanted to apologise. To explain. But he couldn't even explain it to himself. Had he really finally stopped pushing her away in some kind of attempt at reverse psychology on himself? It sounded ludicrous even in his own mind.

Not giving her any chance to stammer any further, Fitz adopted a deliberately breezy tone.

'So plenty of time to test drill for suitable watercourses in each location.'

'Yes, but—'

'And you know as well as I do that this country's health status is one of the worst. Lack of education about defecating near the same rivers from which drinking water is collected is a significant issue, and admittedly the wells are only a small part of it, as is the long-term plan to start building new sewer and wastewater treatment plants.'

'Yes, I know—'

'But the wells will still help, not least in reducing diarrhoea and therefore malnourishment, helminth, typhus, kidney diseases, shall I go on?'

A look of defeat skittered over her face.

'I suppose if you put it like that...' She shrugged.

'It's exactly like that.'

He pushed back his sense of triumph, knowing that he was only trying to deceive himself. Accompanying the medical unit into the local communities was an inspired idea, but it was the knowledge that he would therefore have to accompany her that gave him the greater sense of satisfaction.

The entire situation was alien to Fitz and while he knew he would never compromise a mission, or his role, for Elle, the fact remained that he was more than happy at the prospect of being able to combine the two so easily.

Then again, the thought appeared from nowhere, *how many times had he seen a vehicle flip over in front of or behind him?*

The thought came before he had the chance to check himself.

'Now, whose vehicle would you prefer to travel in?'

She looked aghast.

'Say again?'

'I recommend my four-by-four—it's less of a bumpy ride than your ambulance—but it's your choice.'

She sucked in a breath, actually squaring her shoulders as she glared at him.

'I'm not travelling with the engineers.'

They both knew she meant she wasn't travelling with *him*. He smothered a grin. This was a heck of a lot better than the tension of the last week. It felt like a step back to the easy banter they'd enjoyed that first night in the bar, and he was going to enjoy it fully for the next few minutes.

'Is there a medical priority?' he enquired with wry politeness.

She narrowed her eyes at him, quite aware that he was teasing her.

'You know there isn't. But—'

'Good.' Fitz nodded, ignoring her objection. 'Because we still need to talk about the design variations for the hospital and several hours of driving through nothingness, with nothing else to do, is the ideal opportunity.'

CHAPTER ELEVEN

TWO AND A half hours of pure torture.

Elle squirmed in her seat as the four-by-four finally drew to a halt just outside the buildings of their first local community. It was all she could do not to fling open the door and throw herself out just to get away from Fitz. How was it that in spite of the callous way in which he'd rejected her this last week, she still wanted him? She'd never known it was possible to feel a yearning so intense that it actually physically *hurt.*

And then she'd fallen under his spell all over again. She'd fallen for the idea of something more with him, even if she had precisely zero idea what that would be. Although she was fairly sure it hadn't been being cooped up in the back of a four-by-four with him, jolted around so much that their bodies had been in contact the entire journey, yet unable to talk freely because of the driver.

Really, she should pat herself on the back. For two hours, thirty-one minutes and some seconds she had endured Fitz's solid thigh pressed against her, generating heat that had little to do with the soaring daytime temperatures as it had bounced off each other's bodies, and withstood the sparks of awareness and the tiniest hairs prickling in response. She had spent two hours, thirty-one minutes and some seconds muffling the maddening military tattoo roll over her heart as his deep voice had rumbled into her ear and through her body to ignite a wanton fire in the depth of her core.

And she had forced herself to concentrate on designs and principles and timings for two hours, thirty-one minutes and some seconds, when all her brain had wanted to do was mull over the intoxicating possibilities that his earlier assertions had raised.

She *affected* him. He'd said so. He had rejected and humiliated her, proved to her that he *could* turn it on and off like the twist of a tap, yet her torment was all no longer of her own making.

It had turned out he wasn't so immune to her after all. Even if she still wasn't sure where that left them. When they got back home, did he want to date? Would they be colleagues with benefits? And what did *she* want? Elle wasn't even sure she knew. Realistically, she and Fitz knew so little about each other, perhaps his olive branch to be friends was just about getting to know each other while they were out here.

It was probably a good idea. But one thing she *did* know was that, despite the crushing effect Fitz had on her, she had miraculously found a way to push aside her emotions and discuss steadily, and proficiently, all Fitz's proposed variations to the hospital services layout, even putting forward several improvements of her own. Surprisingly, perhaps even astoundingly, it seemed when it came to working together on their military assignment, she and Fitz made a remarkably strong, united team. A professional team.

She couldn't help liking the idea of that. But just because they had proved once again that they could still work in harmony on a mission level, it didn't give them the green light to make their relationship a sexual one again. Even if her throbbing body was trying to convince her otherwise.

Her internal battle had undoubtedly taken its toll—a battle with her own body, and with her very senses, leaving her mentally and physically spent. As the engines were all finally killed and the occupants began to spill from the various vehicles, Elle opened the door and unfurled her shaky legs, furiously berating her wandering thoughts even as she put some distance between herself and Fitz.

She propelled herself towards the ambulance where the supplies for the community sat ready to go. *This* was what she was here for—helping people, saving lives, health education. In other words, her job as an army doctor. It was what she understood. It was what she was good at.

Reaching for her grab-bag, she slung it over her shoulder and followed their interpreter, and Zi, the sixty-three-year-old widow who had spent nearly a decade volunteering with charities across the border to help educate small villages and communities, and would be working with the army in this region until the charities came in to take over. They were already being eagerly welcomed inside what passed for the community hall, and Elle hurried to catch up. It wasn't always this easy but today of all days she was grateful for the lack of local resistance. Fitz hadn't followed her, his own good grasp of the local language allowing him to quickly begin chatting to some of the local men. He, too, appeared to be meeting very little distrust. If every stop they made was this smooth, they'd be heading back to the hospital in half the time.

Elle's sense of reprieve grew as she looked through the window to see him begin moving around the village to find potential bore sites, and she tasked herself with carrying out the immunisations she was there for. And yet their earlier conversation, his evident thawing towards her, had jump-started previously well-controlled feelings within her, as though the antagonism of the last week was forgotten and they had both been thrown back to the awkward, stumbling yet thrilling feeling of the morning-after-the-night-before.

Not that she'd ever experienced it before for herself, but the way her body was reacting now, like a million teeny-tiny jumping spiders were playing on trampolines in her tummy, it was exactly how she would have imagined it would feel. She felt his presence everywhere, as if the village itself was too small to hold him.

If she'd thought Fitz had got into her head after that first night together, after that incredible sex, after the way he'd made her feel, then it was nothing compared to the way Fitz was cracking open her heart with even the mere hint that he was opening himself up to her on an emotional level.

Looping her stethoscope around her neck, Elle

forced herself to quash the tumbling thoughts and beamed at her team.

'Ready, guys? Let's help to save some kids' lives. Look out for anything else we can help with now—diarrhoea, open wounds, you know the drill. Zi will be chatting to the women in the waiting area about latrines, hand washing, basic hygiene—the women are still going to the toilet in the open air so they'll be the first to get a latrine, but the community's waste is still getting into the river where they draw their drinking water. So let's take any opportunity to back up what Zi will be telling them.

'Also, the community have put forward five or six grandmothers, elders who they respect and listen to, so we'll join Zi in a couple of hours to start taking them through health care, mainly focussing on clean water and sanitation procedures, and pregnancy and labour advice. Anything to help prepare the ground for when the charities start running their full programmes in the coming weeks and months.'

To a chorus of enthusiastic agreement, Elle watched her teams filter out to their cubicles, maximising the number of patients they could see as well as administering the polio and measles immunisations. It was proving to be an interesting mission out here, and each day she was more and more convinced that returning on a second back-to-back tour would be a rewarding, if challenging experience.

The rest of Elle's morning passed in something of a blur. At least she and Jools—the staff sergeant and nurse assisting her with the vaccines—went way back. Jools had been one of Elle's closest allies when Elle had just been a lieutenant and the woman had a razor-sharp wit and an innate skill at drawing the local women into the levity, even if they couldn't understand the precise wording. A morning of laughter was just what she needed and, given the nature of the medical units and their work, rank and title were often shunned in favour of a first-name basis, meaning things were less formal and more easygoing.

So when the first lull came a couple of hours later, Elle couldn't help but balk at the thought of Jools suggesting they take their usual leg-stretching walk to get out of the stifling room for a while.

'Maybe it's time we get a small group together and head out to encourage the villagers to attend clinic,' Elle remarked as they set up a new batch of needles while the last set of patients left the room. 'I know Zi is good, and we've been lucky so far this morning, but there are bound to be more families who haven't come down yet.'

'No need.' Jools grinned. 'Have you seen the waiting area?'

Stepping around the cubicle, Elle carefully peered through before spinning back to her colleague in shock.

'It's full out there. I don't understand.'

What was more, many of the women were grouped attentively around Zi, who was educating them and entertaining the children in one easy performance. It was the lack of noise that had prompted Elle to think there weren't many families out there, but the question still remained as to why, since Zi had been indoors all morning, so many of them had come across voluntarily.

It was never usually this easy. They often had to carefully persuade suspicious members of the male population to allow their wives and children to get immunised. It was easier if the charities had been teaching the respected grandmothers about the benefits so *they* could encourage their sons to do the same, but Elle knew her team was the first in the area for a decade.

'They all just attended of their own volition?'

'Colonel Fitzwilliam,' the nurse said dreamily, as though his name in itself was explanation enough.

'Colonel Fitzwilliam?' echoed Elle.

The whimsical gaze only intensified. Elle gritted her teeth. She'd barely managed to stop herself from watching every time he passed, her eyes seeming to lift up at just the right moment to see his robust form striding across the frame of the tiny window with, even more surprisingly, a growing cluster of village men scurrying eagerly after him. Or to see him setting aside his own work to carry out some manual labour or other with the community, winning hearts and minds by actually joining in with something the village had been working on and needed.

And in those moments Elle had seen exactly how Fitz had acquired, and maintained, that impressive physique of his. Not in a gym but in the real world. Not with artificial machines but doing real manual labour. She'd remembered with embarrassing clarity just how he'd felt, driving inside her, claiming her, imprinting himself on her for ever.

Even at this distance, even though appearing no bigger than a matchstick, Fitz dominated entirely.

'I'm not sure what he has to do with the heaving waiting area.' She hadn't intended to sound so prim.

'Well, that's because not everyone is as immune to charm as you, Major I-Only-Have-Eyes-for-My-Childhood-Sweetheart!' Jools laughed. 'And Major Fitzwilliam has charm in spades. Haven't you seen how he's been working out there with the local men? And on more than just the wells. Last time I went for a new batch of vaccines from the mobile unit I heard that the six-tonner he brought with him was loaded with supplies for building hen-houses. Did you know that?'

'We have some basic kits to get them started!' Elle exclaimed. 'The charities gave them to us and they'll do the rest when they come out. He knew that, he even mentioned it to me this morning.'

'Yes, but the Colonel brought better timber and some tools. He's been showing them how to build them to best suit the birds, and which ground is better for siting them. He's been gaining their trust and apparently casually chatting to them about the health benefits of the clinic.'

'So that heaving waiting area is *his* doing?'

'Amazing, isn't he?' Jools sighed. 'I'd love to have your job as liaison officer, having to work with him practically every day and on a one-on-one basis. Getting to travel that awful journey out here cooped up with him. No offence but it's wasted on you.'

Elle resisted the urge to roll her eyes. *How could she criticise Jools's swooning when she herself wasn't much different?*

'Wait, look, he's about to send over some more. A couple of local men just approached him and pointed over here. You'll see.'

Her legs almost carried her back to the window of their own volition as Elle spotted Fitz conferring with his newfound supporters, nodding in agreement as they gesticulated towards her location. Even the interpreter didn't seem to need to do much translating. Moments later, the men crossed the ground and went into various homes or out of sight.

'Give it a few minutes and a group of fresh families will come through our doors,' Jools confirmed. 'There, that's the last of this batch of immunisations set up. Shall I have the next group readied for us?'

'Sure,' Elle replied, still staring thoughtfully

through the window at the apparent hero of the hour. 'The quicker we can get through them, the sooner we can move on to help the next village.'

Thanks to Fitz, it seemed they might be able to get to even more communities and help even more locals during this trip.

It was bad enough lusting after the guy, but did he have to make her admire him so much, too?

She needed to get through the next couple of days and then she'd be back at the hospital and could go back to avoiding him. So much for wanting the chill between them to thaw. It seemed that, instead of helping matters, his new openness to her had only confused matters and made her all the more attracted to him.

Clearly, in future, she needed to watch what she wished for.

'There you are. I wondered where you were hiding out.'

Elle clutched her ration-pack hot chocolate in its steel cup—watery and tasteless, but at least wet and welcoming—as the dust storm raged outside. For two days the sky had been perfectly blue as they'd travelled from village to village, some makeshift, some well established. Thanks to Fitz and Zi, they had encountered less resistance than normal and had therefore been able to do more than normal, successfully immunising children, health-checking pregnant mothers and passing on even more valuable sensitisation information than previously planned. Elle had even convinced herself that they would get back to the hospital before the weather turned.

Murphy's law, however, meant that the storm hit just as her team had been loading up the last of their kit. Still, she supposed it was better than if they'd been halfway between two locations and slap-bang in the middle of nowhere. At least this was one of the largest established communities and they had shelter, a safe place to wait it out.

At least, it *had* been safe before *he'd* walked through the door.

'I'm not hiding out,' she lied.

'The rest of the two teams are in the main community hall across the square.'

'And I'd have been with them if I hadn't been packing up the last of my kit when the storm came out of nowhere.'

'I think we both know you had time to get across, if you'd wanted to.'

Elle dipped her head and took another sip of the

watery drink. He was right, there was little point in denying it.

'You were avoiding me.'

There was a beat of silence.

'Can you blame me?'

'I thought we'd decided on starting afresh. No antagonism.'

'I know.' Elle rubbed her forehead. 'I'm just… not sure how to be around you. I've never been in this situation before.'

'Neither have I,' he said wryly, turning his back to her and unpacking a small gas stove from his pack.

She watched as he lit it, the flickering flame instantly changing the atmosphere in the low-lit room, and she couldn't help it, she was transported back to that bar the first night.

'Here, try this instead.'

His voice cut into her thoughts as he replaced the cup in her hands with something that felt decidedly more…luxurious. As the decadent scent reached her nostrils she bit back her objection and sniffed appreciatively.

'It's not five-star-hotel hot chocolate,' he murmured. 'But it's better than that ration-pack sludge you were drinking.'

He remembered. The drink she'd ordered when they'd got room service in the early hours. It was such a tiny point but the fact that he'd noted it, and echoed it now, was touching. She couldn't stop it. For an instant she was transported back to that night. Being in this tiny dark, supply room of the stone building, so utterly basic yet the village's beloved town hall, was hardly the same as the relative opulence of her hotel room. And yet they were alone again, and she couldn't help feeling oddly safe. Just as she had with him that first night.

She could keep fighting it, but the attraction wasn't going away.

Her head snapped up to meet his gaze, unprepared for the hard, heated look in his eyes. Dizziness threatened to overtake her and she told herself it was just hunger from the mayhem of the last few days.

She knew that wasn't it.

'I'm still not entirely sure what it is that we're starting over,' she confessed.

If she'd expected him to prevaricate she'd been wrong. He snagged her gaze, pinning her in place, his voice clear, confident.

'Getting to know each other.'

'To what end?'

'Whatever we decide.'

'Okay,' she managed. 'Starting with what?'

'Tell me about Stevie. How you let him hurt you.'

'Low blow,' she muttered.

'Not intentionally.' Fitz shook his head. 'You just don't seem like the type to stand for any nonsense, and yet the things you've told me suggest otherwise.'

'You mean...the sex.' She flushed, thinking of their conversation that first night when Fitz had dropped to his knees and pressed his lips to her sex. And so much more.

'I mean the sex, the cheating. I got the impression you weren't surprised, so I'm guessing it wasn't the first time.'

God, had he really read all that as easily as if she'd been an open book?

She didn't intend to sound defensive, but that was how it came out.

'I suppose you think I was stupid to stay with him?'

'I don't think anything, that's why I'm asking.'

She bit her lip in discomfort, not understanding why it was so important to him.

'Tell me, why do you want to play detective all of a sudden?'

'It isn't all of a sudden,' he muttered. 'I wanted to know from the start.'

The irritation in his tone caught her attention. It wasn't so much that he wanted to know, she realised, as that he *had* to know. He couldn't fathom her and he was intrigued. Which meant he cared. More than he was prepared to admit.

She inhaled deeply, formed her mouth into a perfect O and blew out. Then flashed a bitter, humourless smile. 'The ten-thousand-pound question.'

'You stayed with him for ten thousand pounds?' Fitz's face twisted into a mix of expressions she couldn't identify but which she could easily guess.

'You could put it like that if you like.'

'I don't like.' His jaw locked in irritation and it surprised her that she was beginning to recognise his 'tells' so easily. 'So explain it to me.'

She sighed.

'What would be the point? Apart from satisfying your curiosity? Would it change anything between us? Not, I realise, that there *is* an us.'

'Humour me, Elle.'

She thought for a long time, then dipped her head.

'Short version only.'

'Whatever you prefer. For now.'

She chose to ignore that.

'Stevie and I were childhood sweethearts. I was fourteen, he was fifteen, though we'd known each other all our lives. We were both poor kids from the worst housing estate in the area, but while his dad baled on his mum and her seven kids, my parents were the exception. I can't remember a day when they didn't have a laugh with each other, a joke, a hug, a tease.'

'They never argued?'

The look in his eyes was so fleeting, so inscrutable that Elle wasn't sure if it had simply been her imagination.

'Yeah, they argued. Of course they did. We had no money, and that always created tension. But they always made it up. Every single night. They told us kids we should never go to bed in anger. She was so beautiful, my mum, deep red hair and sparkling green eyes.'

'Like you,' Fitz said softly.

She snorted, trying to conceal how his words affected her.

'No, not like me. I have her basic components, but I'm not stunning like she was.'

'*Just* like your mother,' he murmured again.

He held her gaze and it took everything she had to tear her eyes away.

'And they danced, God, how they loved to dance. They could jive and swing and lindy hop like you wouldn't believe.'

'You told me you couldn't dance that night in the bar.'

She flushed, recalling the feel of Fitz's arms around her, his fingers grazing her skin, his thigh slotted between hers. She swallowed. Hard.

'I can't. It was one of their greatest sources of amusement. But they could and they used to enter competitions and I'd go and watch. Stevie too. The kids around where we lived had no prospects, there was no such thing as a school night, and their idea of recreation was going around the back of the station to drink cider and take drugs...'

'*Their* idea of recreation? Not yours?'

'No. I dreamed of becoming a doctor. Don't ask me where it came from, even my parents never knew, but apparently it started from the age of about five and it was all I ever wanted to be when I grew up. And Stevie, he had his football and he dreamed of making it his way out of that hell-hole too.'

'So you and he bonded over being different.'

'Sure, why not?' Elle frowned at his scepticism. 'We were the outliers. The oddballs who didn't fit in. When my mother died, my father was so lonely that he remarried. I think he was trying recapture what he'd lost with Mum, but it wasn't the same. She was cruel, but I suppose when I look back she was jealous of what my parents had had. But Stevie was there. Back then he was loyal, and kind, and generous. He kept telling me to fight for my dream even when she was nasty and told me I had ideas above my station. She told me I was wasting my time getting A Levels when I'd never be able to afford university anyway. She tried to make me get a job in the local factory—everyone got a job in the local factory—and bring a wage in instead of scrounging off her.'

'But you got to uni. You joined the army and got a scholarship and did it by yourself.'

'No.' Elle shook her head. 'I didn't. She was right, I couldn't afford university. I didn't know the army gave bursaries for medical degrees and I knew I didn't stand a hope in hell of making it through. But by then Stevie had made it to professional league football and he wouldn't let me give up on my dream. He used his money and he paid for my degree, my accommodation, my books, my food, he paid for everything.'

'As long as you turned a blind eye to his cheating?'

'No. Not back then. I'm sure of it. The old Stevie wasn't like that. Oh, I don't know. Maybe he did. He certainly never gave me a key to his place in all those years, and I never just turned up apart from that last time. His doorman recognised me and let me in.'

'So he *did* cheat on you.'

'Maybe. But, God, Fitz, you have to understand, we were two kids from nothing. And he was suddenly catapulted into this world where he was idolised. Seems like everybody loves a footballer when they're winning. He had fans, groupies, people who adored him, and he was nineteen with no home life to speak of to keep him grounded. Is it any wonder he let the fame and adulation get to him?'

Fitz sneered.

'You're seriously making excuses for him?'

'No,' she cried. 'I'm the last person who would do that. I'm just saying I can see how it happened. And I wonder if I couldn't have been the one thing to keep him steady…if I'd only cared enough to try. But I didn't. I didn't care enough and I didn't try. We never saw each other, between his training and his matches he didn't have much spare time, and by then I'd got an army bursary and I didn't want to make the time either. So he was pretty much on his own, surrounded by sycophants and girls throwing themselves at him. The cheating started after that and things deteriorated year on year.'

'Yet you still didn't leave?'

'Like I said, I felt guilty.' Elle shrugged. 'Not guilty enough to make an effort, but guilty enough not to leave. I didn't want the responsibility of ending things. I think I was waiting for him to do it. When it all boils down to it, I still felt as though I owed him, that without his help that first year I would never have become a doctor.'

'You'd have found another way.'

'Maybe.' She shrugged. 'But we'll never know. Stevie made sure I never had to risk that.'

'If he was so great, why didn't you love him?'

'I never said he was so great. He was impossibly moody, and he had his father's temper. And I did love him, in the beginning. But it was teenage love, tainted by where we grew up. We got together through circumstance, we were never a good fit. And Stevie was a brilliant footballer but…well, we could never have what you might call an in-depth conversation. If it wasn't about football or movies then forget it.'

'But when he cheated, you still felt guilty?'

'Don't underestimate guilt, Fitz. It can tie you up in knots. You can't understand what it's like.'

'I can,' he muttered unexpectedly. 'More than you think.'

'Your mother and sister?' she guessed hesitantly. 'Or Janine?'

The room was so thick with tension Elle thought the dust storm might as well have entered the building.

'What have you heard about her?'

'Not a lot,' Elle confessed. 'But you're an eligible male around the site. You know what gossip is like. I heard she was a logistics officer and you were once engaged?'

It took a long time before he broke the silence.

'It's complicated.'

'Try me,' Elle asked.

He shook his head but she couldn't let it drop. It was about more than just words.

'Trust me. Please, Fitz. Like I just trusted you.'

This time he didn't reply. The silence in the

compact space grew, slowly but surely seeming to suck all the oxygen out of the room until Elle felt she was on the verge of suffocating. When he finally opened his mouth to speak, to break the spell, it wasn't with a murmur but with a growl that seemed to explode in her head.

The sound of a door banging open in the main room outside, interrupting with an urgency that was impossible to ignore, had them both leaping to their feet.

A pregnant young woman, crying out and bloodied, was being carried in by an older man, flanked by at least four others, a long shard of metal debris impaled through the side of her abdomen.

CHAPTER TWELVE

'GET THE INTERPRETER,' Elle instructed quickly as she hurried forward, trying to encourage them to bring the girl through to a gurney.

'No need.'

Grimly Fitz matched her, communicating efficiently with the group as Elle struggled to make out snippets and words in the cacophony of voices. Back and forth the conversation went as Fitz quickly established order, instructing them to bring the woman through to where Elle could examine her and eliciting information.

His face tightened.

'What's wrong?' Elle pressed urgently.

'She's seven months pregnant, and they were travelling on the main road out there when the storm hit. They pulled over to wait it out but another car coming in the opposite direction drove off the road and into them, rolling their car down an embankment into the wadi at the side.'

Elle drew her lips into a thin line, remembering

the route from the way in. It was a fair way down, the car could have rolled a couple of times and she doubted the woman had been wearing a seatbelt.

'She's in pain and afraid for the baby.'

His voice broke on the last part and Elle stared at him in shock. His expression was too haunted, too bleak to be solely a reaction to this woman's condition. But there was no time for her to dwell on it. Her priority was the woman and her baby.

'Can you send one of the men to the main building, ask for Jools, and tell her to bring my medical bag?'

'I'll go. I can't send anyone out there,' Fitz managed, his voice filled with pain like nothing she'd ever heard from him before.

Something in her heart broke for him, even if she didn't know why.

'No. I need you here to translate.' Elle stopped him firmly.

He moved to the door, not appearing to hear her.

'Colonel.' She raised her voice firmly. 'Colonel Fitzwilliam. *Fitz.*'

He finally turned at her last bellow.

'You cannot go, do you understand?' Elle said quietly but firmly. 'You need to listen to me, this is a medical situation.'

For a moment she wasn't sure her words were registering, and then he snapped out of it—whatever it was—as quickly as it had started.

'Major,' he acknowledged, turning to the men and issuing the instruction.

There was little need for discussion as two of them promptly volunteered and headed out together. Elle was relieved; there was a degree of safety in numbers. Quickly Elle moved on, turning back to the woman and tapping her own chest as she gave her name, smiling when the woman responded in kind.

'Roshan, good, that's good.' So at least the woman was cognisant enough to process Elle's words.

Her language skills might not be anywhere as fluent as Fitz's, but the army had given her plenty of phrases to assist in everyday and medical situations.

'Colonel,' Elle stated, more to establish order than anything else, 'can you ask the men for their accounts of what happened while I ask Roshan here? Get as much information as possible.'

There was no time now to think about Fitz, but something had spooked him and she didn't think it was just about the crash. She could feel emotion flowing off Fitz, hot then cold, colourless then vivid, still then raging. It seeped into her chest, pulling it tight, and it seeped into her head, making it feel ready to explode. A mass of contradictions, out of control. A mess. And nothing like the man Elle knew. She struggled to make sense of it and then, all of a sudden, it hit her.

Pain.

This was what Fitz had been stuffing down all this time. The barrier that had always stood between them. The wall she'd wanted him to tear down for as long as she could remember. The trench that had stopped him from trusting her, and which had made her feel as though she ought to think it was too soon after Stevie. But finally she couldn't ignore the truth any longer. She was falling for Fitz. She'd probably started falling for him from the minute they'd met.

Fitz had been everything Stevie hadn't been. She'd spent years acknowledging all the ways that Stevie wasn't the right man for her, so when Fitz had come along she—or at least a part of her subconscious—had recognised in an instant all the qualities she knew she wanted in a man.

And now he was hurting and all she wanted to do was help, but there wasn't time. She'd have to get to the bottom of it. Later. With a supreme effort, Elle pushed thoughts of Fitz from her mind and turned back to Roshan to ask where it hurt most and if there had been any blood. Despite the long metal shard in her abdomen, Elle conducted a quick visual triage knowing that the most obvious injury wasn't always the most life-threatening.

As she finished, the interpreter hurried in with Jools. By the looks of them, the worst of the dust storm had passed, but that didn't mean they were free and clear.

'That looks bad. But then again, there isn't much blood,' the interpreter muttered quietly to her. 'What do you want me to tell her?'

'Nothing at the moment. There's no way to know merely by looking. The lack of blood doesn't prove anything. She's breathing and talking, and she's gesticulating so that's good and I want to do a full primary check, but first I'd like to make sure she has no other injuries, specifically neck and back, and what state that penetrating injury is in, so that I can get her onto her left side.'

'They keep telling her to stay on her back.'

'Yes, I can see that, but I need you to explain that uterine compression on the inferior vena cava and aorta can aggravate shock in pregnant women, especially if they're in the third trimester. Put it into whatever terms you need to in order to make them understand.'

She waved Fitz over. A darkness swirled in his eyes, almost mesmerising. But it seemed he still wasn't going to speak. Elle stared in silence, feeling herself being drawn into their dangerous depths. She could drown in those depths and never realise it.

'Can you get me a kit bag from the medical vehicle, blood-pressure monitor, blankets and maybe some kind of screen? Okay.' Elle turned her focus to the mother with a soothing tone. 'Let's look after you.'

There was no point telling the woman everything would be all right. Although there was no evidence of vaginal bleeding or significant external bleeding from the penetration wound, Elle had no idea what was going on inside. The shard may or may not have caused direct trauma to the foetus, ruptured the placenta, damaged organs or caused internal bleeding. Yet the initial check was looking more positive than she'd feared.

By the time Fitz had returned with the bag, Elle was satisfied the woman's pulse was strong, she wasn't clammy or pale, and from the way she was describing the accident, frequently punctuated by sharp pleas to make sure her baby was all right, she didn't seem confused or weak in any way.

'What now?' Fitz appeared suddenly at her shoulder, his voice uncharacteristically tight.

'At this point I'm as satisfied as I can be that Roshan isn't going into hypovolemic shock. Neitherr does she indicate any kind of abdominal pain, even from the metal shard. Now I can only hope the penetration wound isn't as deep as I'd feared, but we still need to pack her carefully for moving her.'

'You're moving her?' Fitz didn't look happy.

'With that shard in her side, I want to check the baby's well-being then do a secondary check on the mother. We'll have to get them to our hospital, Razorwire's too far away or I'd call it in.'

'If the baby's alive, will you need to operate? To save it?'

'A C-section? Not necessarily,' Elle answered grimly. 'Besides, until the hospital is up and running we have no incubators or anything to help. We don't even have the new generators yet. But it's too soon to tell what Roshan or her baby might need.'

Slipping in the earpieces of her portable foetal heart monitor just in case, Elle prepared herself as she searched for the heartbeat, her eyes locked to the screen. It was almost a shock when she found it, slightly slower than she would have preferred but strong and steady.

Clicking for a printout, Elle removed the earphones so that the woman could hear the sound of her baby for herself. She was rewarded with a flood of tears from the mother.

'It's alive,' Fitz bit out.

'Yes, not in any immediate distress.'

'Then you're leaving the metal *in situ*?'

'I'd prefer to, yes,' she confirmed, knowing he would understand that from combat injuries. 'At the moment it doesn't appear to be causing an issue and we'll have more on hand back at the hospital, if anything goes wrong.'

'So now?'

'Now we make sure everyone else is okay.'

'Already done. Jools and your team have taken the rest over to the other building. It's calm outside now. They'll deal with everyone and we've got anyone who needs further attention onto appropriate vehicles. Most look to be only superficial injuries, the only vehicle really damaged was the one carrying the woman and her husband and he has a head wound she wants you to look at.'

'Great.' Elle nodded, those black depths drawing her in again.

She struggled to break free. She *would* drown, that was the point, because Fitz would never throw her a lifeline. Not because he didn't want to but because somehow he didn't think he could. At least, not in his personal life. In his professional life as a leader Fitz not only lived up to but exceeded his responsibilities—she'd seen that for herself over the last couple of weeks. But in his personal life he appeared to have some ridiculous notion that he destroyed life, destroyed people. *He* was the one who needed a lifeline, and Elle couldn't shake the belief that she was the only one who could offer it to him.

'What was that about, Fitz?' she asked softly.

'It was nothing.'

'I see.'

She didn't push it immediately. His very choice of words acknowledged there had been something even as he tried to deny it. She let his unintentional admission sink into his own head.

'It was nothing you should have to be concerned with.'

'If it affects you,' she answered simply, 'I'm concerned.'

She knew he held himself responsible for his mother's death, and his sister's death, even though he hadn't been there. She knew, too, that he held himself responsible for Janine's convoy accident, even though he couldn't possibly have had any influence over it. He was Royal Engineers, she'd been Logistics. None of it seemed to make sense, but the worst of it was that Fitz didn't trust anyone—didn't trust *her*—enough to confide in her.

And that hurt more than anything else.

Worse, because she knew she had no right to expect him to want to confide in her, but it didn't stop her wishing he wanted to. It didn't stop her falling for him.

Working with him over the last couple of months twenty-four seven had been eye-opening. In a job like this, especially in an environment like this, Elle knew only too well how soldiers got to know the people working alongside them in a way no other profession allowed. They lived together, ate together, slept together. There was no escape, no chance to step away for a while.

It had also meant she'd spent more days in Fitz's company than she'd spent with Stevie in probably the last five or six years they'd been together. And she liked the man Fitz was more than she'd ever liked the man Stevie had been turning into.

She couldn't help it. She wanted to be there for Fitz, she wanted to show him he needed her. And he *did* need her. Hadn't he already told her things he'd admitted he'd never told anyone else? Their connection was real, she wasn't imagining it. It wasn't just about the sex that first night.

Fitz spent the entire journey back oscillating between relief and frustration. Relief at the fact that Elle was in the ambulance with Roshan, giving him some much-needed breathing room, and frustration at the realisation that only Elle's presence next to him would have calmed his uncharacteristically jangling nerves.

He'd been shocked when she'd mentioned Janine, but the anger he might have previously expected to flood out of him had gone, replaced by a deep-seated need to talk it through with someone. With Elle.

It was almost torture when she disappeared into the hospital with Roshan and he had to return to his office alone, searching for paperwork to occupy his racing thoughts. Yet at the same time he was immensely grateful to her for saving both the young mum's life and that of her baby. As if some-how it made up for the baby he and Janine had lost.

He had no idea how much time passed until a light knock on his door wrestled him from his dark thoughts.

'I thought you might like to know mother and baby are resting and are fine. I eventually removed the shard and incredibly it had missed the baby en-tirely and slid into a void between Roshan's inter-nal organs. They both handled the operation well and I'm hoping she'll be able to carry her baby to term.'

'How likely is that?'

'If they get through the night without any com-plications, I'll be a lot happier,' Elle admitted. 'Be-sides, the generators are due in the next few days, and as soon as we have them up and running the first incubators will arrive. If Roshan can at least hang on until then, it would be great.'

He took in her wan smile, the strain around her eyes giving her away.

'You must be exhausted,' he said quietly. 'Thank you for coming to tell me.'

She blinked.

'I thought you were going to…talk to me.'

Part of him wanted to. Another part thought he'd dodged that bullet for today.

'I thought you might prefer to get some sleep. I can't imagine you've had more than about ten hours over the last four days or so.'

'Right,' Elle conceded stiffly.

Still, she hesitated as though she wanted to say more. Instead, finally, she dipped her head and stepped towards the door. He should be grateful that she wasn't trying to push the matter.

'Janine was my ex-fiancée,' he announced abruptly, watching as she froze with her hand on the doorhandle. Slowly, so slowly, she drew her fingers back, listening to him without turning around. 'Not that I think you can call it an engagement really. It lasted less than twenty-four hours and it wasn't exactly planned. There was a baby.'

She twisted her head back over her shoulder.

'I don't understand.'

He didn't blame her. He wasn't sure even he had ever understood it, everything had happened so fast.

'Janine was a fellow officer. We met at Sandhurst. She was kind and generous and quiet, exactly the kind of girl I ought to like. To love. She understood the army and she loved me. I wanted to love her back.'

'You wanted to?'

He could hear the confusion in her voice.

'There was no reason why I shouldn't have loved her. I liked her. But that was it. I couldn't. That was when I realised I was flawed. I'm not like other people, Elle, I don't feel the way other people do. I lack that empathy, that connection.'

'I don't believe that. You just weren't right for each other.'

'No, you don't understand. I felt more for Janine than I have any other person but I couldn't love her. It just wasn't there. I was selfish, just like my father was.'

He watched her expression change from surprise, to shock, to disbelief.

'You are *not* your father. How could you even think that?'

Her faith in him was humbling, the way her eyes stared so deeply into his as if she could somehow show him exactly how she saw him.

But he had to resist. He couldn't fall for it. She knew about his cruel and violent father, she understood about the car crash, she soothed his guilt over not being there for his mother and sister. However, she didn't know about Janine.

And it was time he told her. He owed Elle that much. That hard, unwieldy truth.

'Elle,' he began, 'I don't deserve your kindness. I never did. You think I'm a better man that I am. I wish you were right, but you're not.'

'Fitz—'

'No.' He stood up, cutting her off before she could object. 'You keep insisting I'm this stand-up guy because that's the army guy everyone sees. But you're wrong. All of you. The man I seem to be able to be out here is the person I would like to be. The colonel I would like to be. I like who I am, what I've achieved, how much my men accomplish when inspired. It's why I love my job. I've poured everything I have into my career.'

'I know that,' she began, but he refused to let her steer the conversation.

'But I'm not that same man back home, out of Green, in my personal life. I never have been. God knows, I've tried.'

'You *are* the same man. I saw it that night. You're just too plagued with the demons of your past to see it. You signed up within weeks of that fatal car crash and you used the army to give you a new life, to reinvent yourself. And it worked, but in doing so you never allowed yourself time to grieve. I don't think you ever properly grieved. So every time you go home you're still stuck in the same place. Until you grieve you can't let go, and until you let go you can never let yourself move on.'

Every one of her words slammed into him, like rounds into body armour. He wanted to believe her. But he still hadn't told her everything. He sucked in a sharp breath.

'Elle, stop talking for a minute,' he said simply. 'You need to listen, *really* listen, to what I need to tell you.'

He didn't know why, but he began to move around the desk as she stepped closer. As if it was just him and her. And soon the ugly truth.

A sharp rap on the door startled them both.

'Come in.' It was an effort to conceal his frustration.

'Colonel, we've just had a message from Major Howes. There's a problem with one of his troops in the Zenghar Valley. He's caught up with a complication at the railhead after the earthquake.'

The switch was immediate for Fitz. It had to be serious if Carl was calling at this hour.

'The troop out there was building a bridge to link the railhead with this hospital.'

'Yes, sir. They think the earthquake has affected the stability of the ground. Major Howes says there's a large local population who live beneath.'

The risk of landslides in that region was already quite high without the additional danger of the aftershocks.

'Potential for multiple fatalities if the ground gives way...' he muttered, almost to himself.

'We understand so, Colonel.'

'Get me Brigade, Corporal,' Fitz ordered quickly, his mind already engaging.

'They're already on the line, sir. In the ops office.'

He didn't hesitate. He was heading out of the door behind the young lad before he remembered Elle, and spun around quickly.

'We *will* talk,' he said quietly, knowing the corporal was too far away to hear.

'Forget it.' She shook her head, as though it didn't matter in the slightest, though he'd seen the initial frustration in her eyes to match his. 'Go.'

Without another glance, he went.

CHAPTER THIRTEEN

'WELL, THAT WAS a really good morning.' Elle congratulated her team with deliberate brightness as they deposited their theatre gloves and gowns in the bins. 'Three back-to-back surgeries, and all of them went better than anyone could have anticipated. Nice work, guys.'

It felt good to have such a high mood after the last couple of days. Elle reached for the hand scrub, content to listen to the chattering of her colleagues. The storm had caused a fair amount of damage in communities far and wide and injury levels had spiked, but it finally felt like they were starting to break the back of the influx of new arrivals without compromising care for existing patients.

Stepping through the doors to the main corridor to check on the wards, Elle knew instantly that something was wrong. The low, tense buzz was unsettling and it didn't take her long to find Jools, already huddled in conversation with a small group.

'What's going on?'

There was no need for preamble, they knew each other too well. Jools's head snapped up in dismay.

'There's been a landslide in the Zenghar Valley. That earthquake we had the other day was closer to them than to us and they think it likely caused the slide. Razorwire are sending out Medical Emergency Response Teams, but there are sixty-three confirmed dead so far.'

Fitz.

A chilling fear stole through Elle, its icy fingers closing painfully tightly in her chest. That was where one of his other units was bridge-building.

'Colonel Fitzwilliam was heading out there to oversee things.'

Jools nodded grimly.

'The engineers were caught in it, too. We know they suffered a couple of fatalities, but that's all we know.'

Elle didn't understand how her jellified legs didn't buckle under her weight. She wasn't certain how she made it across the room and around the curtain to collapse in the chair, away from prying eyes. She couldn't even be sure how her heart remembered to keep beating after initially hanging, frozen in her chest.

What a time to finally realise she was as invested in Fitz as her parents had once been in each other. As though she'd suddenly discovered that tiny last piece of who she was when she hadn't known, all these years, that a piece of her had been missing. And now, at the fear that Fitz had been injured— or worse—it felt like that tiny, new part of her had just been smashed against an invisible wall and was, even now, shattering into tiny, irreparable fragments inside her. She knew she'd begun to care for him, but when had she begun to care so very deeply?

When had she fallen in love with Fitz?

The stark realisation came out of nowhere.

As insane as it was, a part of her had fallen for him that first night. When he'd been happy to take direction from her with the seizure yet had been able to pre-empt all her needs. When he'd opened up about his family dying in the car crash and she'd seen that very first hint of vulnerability.

Fitz had exuded self-assurance, determination and power right from the start. And it had excited and enthralled her; more than that it had intoxicated her. Yet she'd also seen kindness in him, and been privileged enough to glimpse a sensitivity that had intrigued her. Fitz was everything that Stevie wasn't.

Everything she'd dreamed a life partner would be.

And she'd been prepared to let him slip through her fingers without even trying to fight for him, simply because convention suggested her break-up was too recent and Fitz had to be a rebound. Because she'd allowed Stevie's betrayal to remind her of all the mental blows she'd absorbed from her stepmother as a kid, and she'd forgotten to tell herself that she deserved a love that was better than any of that.

It was time she stopped listening to her head and tried listening to her heart.

She leapt up from the chair and rounded the curtain so fast that she almost collided with another body.

'Elle? Where are you hurrying off to?' Jools gasped as she darted backwards.

'To contact Colonel Duggan at Razorwire,' Elle called over her shoulder as she jogged away. 'They're going to need doctors on the ground and I'm a damn sight more use out there than I am here right now.'

'Good.' Pushing off the wall, Jools raced to catch up. 'Then can you count me in, too.'

'Just leave it be,' Fitz grumbled as he tried to snag his arm away from the young medic. 'I'm fine.'

'You need medical attention, Colonel.' The lance corporal stared him down, though his Adam's apple bobbed nervously. 'Given the nature of your injuries, you need to be easing the strain on your body. The fact that you've just single-handedly pulled three people out of the rubble only means the risk of internal injuries is also a factor.'

Fitz glowered. The boy had guts, he'd give him that. He might only be a lance corporal but he knew that in medical matters he had the authority to dictate to a colonel and, boy, was the kid sticking to his guns. He suppressed a smile of admiration.

'With an attitude like that, remind me to tell your CO that you deserve a field promotion,' he muttered as he settled back on the makeshift gurney. 'Just stitch me up and let me get back to my men.'

'Thank you, sir, but you understand you need to be on a MERT back to Razorwire? You can't put any more physical stress on your body.'

'The MERTs have higher priority patients to

evacuate than me. I'm walking and talking. I'm fine.'

'Like I said, *Colonel*, we don't know about internal injuries...'

'Son,' Fitz growled abruptly, glancing over to where the latest MERT was landing and teams were already ferrying stretchered patients across the ground. They really needed more trained medical staff on the ground, there were so many injured. 'I'm fine. Now, fix me up as quickly as you can so that I can head back to help my men.'

'Sir...' the boy began, then shifted his glance as soon as he caught sight of Fitz's expression. 'Yes, sir.'

Whatever else the lance corporal might have been about to say was lost on Fitz as his eyes locked on one of the disembarking soldiers.

She couldn't be out here.

Before the medic could finish attending to him Fitz had pushed off the gurney and was striding across the ground, barely even paying attention to his step as he moved past the debris littered all around. As though he couldn't get to her fast enough. As though he was running through the thickest, stickiest treacle.

'What the hell are you doing here?'

'Good to see you too, Colonel,' she muttered, as

he realised he'd roared at her, his nose only inches from hers.

He forced himself to lower his voice, though it wasn't as though anyone else could have heard them in the fracas, but he couldn't feel any remorse. Fear splintered through him like an axe cleaving wood, and with it a sense of protectiveness so fierce it was overwhelming, chasing everything else from his head—the landslide, the mission, the chaos around them.

'You can't be here.'

Fitz couldn't explain it, but he felt desperate, panicked, out of control.

Just like he had when he'd finally listened to his mother's terrified messages that night.

He told himself he couldn't see someone else he cared about getting hurt. Because however much he'd tried to dodge it over the last couple of months, he cared about Elle. Deep down, he suspected that was barely scratching the surface of it but he refused to follow that line of thought to its inevitable conclusion. He blinked as he realised she was answering him.

'I'm a trauma doctor.' Outwardly she looked the picture of calm, but he could hear the quiver in her voice. 'And this is an accident site. Where else would I be?'

'You should be back at the hospital. You have patients.'

A silent voice was urging him to send her back where it was safer. Back where even more of the valley couldn't come crashing down over her any second. It had always been a treacherous valley but now no one could be sure exactly how much damage the aftershocks of that earthquake had caused. But that wasn't his call, he wasn't her CO. And thank God, because if he had been, this was exactly why a relationship between them would have been against the rules.

'I should be right here. The relief in place are already taking over in the hospital, and I'm one of Colonel Duggan's first choices to be out here.'

'It isn't safe.' He heard the agony in his words as they were torn from his lips.

Yet the bedlam around them—the confusion that he was here to get a handle on and to calm—was nothing compared to the maelstrom raging deep within his chest right now.

'And that's our job,' she finished softly.

Quiet but steadfast, determined, her jaw set and shoulders squared, ready to stand off against even him if he got in the way of her doing her job. Every inch the professional, driven Elle he'd seen that first night. The Elle he'd so admired, been so drawn to, so attracted to. For several long seconds they stood immobile, and Fitz had the peculiar sensation of everything receding around them.

All the chaos, and the noise, and the dust fell away. It was just him and Elle.

And he finally allowed his brain to acknowledge what his heart and soul had realised a long time ago.

He loved her.

The urge to tell her almost crushed him.

Beautiful, lovely Elle, who always looked for the upside. And if there wasn't one then she created it just by her vibrant spirit and sheer force of will. She was like his morning coffee, like food, like *air*. He'd felt as though he'd almost been holding his breath until he'd seen her each day, and never in his life had he felt such a compulsion to be with someone.

Elle was a woman like no other he'd ever known. The more he knew her, the more he felt he didn't know enough. He wanted to know everything about her, tell her everything about him. He would never get enough of her, this woman who had shone a warm light into even the blackest caverns of his soul.

A woman who resisted the army chefs' chocolate cake if she'd been working in the hospital all day, but could devour two slices if she'd been rushing around the local communities. The woman who loathed drinking her water from a round plastic bottle and always decanted it into a battered square one she refused to throw away. Who had a pink lion token on her pack so she could identify it day or night but had learned a funny little story in the local language to break the ice with the local kids. He knew she always loaded up one of the pockets of her vest with small colouring books and crayons for them.

The thought of losing her actually twisted inside his gut and the urge to tell her almost crushed him.

But this wasn't the place and it certainly wasn't the time.

She was right, it *was* their job out here, and he had always prided himself on his professionalism as an army officer. But more than that, it was who they both were. They'd both chosen this life, they both loved this life and, right now, that had to come first. Besides, Elle's role was certainly vital but there was one thing in his favour.

The noise and pandemonium of their surroundings suddenly raced back to the foreground, crowding in on them.

'Fine.' Fitz blew out a breath. 'But since we aren't back at the hospital and this is *my* site, this is now *my* command. You listen to me, understand?'

'Colonel.' She dipped her head in acknowledgement, a soft smile playing on her lips as the light he so loved tiptoed back into her eyes. 'So where would you like me?'

He thrust the last of his doubts and fear away.

'What have you got? A couple of twelve by twelves?'

'Three of them, so far.'

It took him seconds to glance around the site, years of experience kicking in. There was a decent location a few hundred metres away, safe enough to be out of line of immediate danger but close enough that the injured could be easily carried there to be triaged, treated or prepped for the MERTs, and close to the helicopter landing site.

'You can set up over there.'

'Yes, Colonel,' Elle agreed, snatching her pack up and spinning back around to where her team was offloading kit from the helicopter. He watched her go, irrationally proud of the woman he saw; a woman who was liked and respected everywhere she went.

A woman who had achieved the one thing he'd never expected anyone could ever do so subtly he hadn't even noticed it happening; she'd put the shattered fragments of his heart back together and, more than that, she'd done so with such skill that he almost couldn't believe it had ever been crushed in the first place.

In his life there had been a few people who had known about what had happened to his mother and his sister. The therapist the state had made him visit for that first week before he'd turned eighteen, the army mental health doctor when he'd enlisted a couple of weeks later, even Janine when her father had told her what was in his file about the crash, but he'd never told them some of the things he'd told Elle that first night.

And although all of them had told him it hadn't been his fault, none of them had made him believe it. None of them had known the full story that Elle had known, about the phone messages or the abuse his mother had suffered. Elle had been the one to make him accept that he couldn't have changed anything. That he couldn't have known his mother was calling because his father had reappeared after three years, and that even if he'd raced home after that first call they would already have been gone. Even if he'd called the police, no one could have got there in time.

She'd allowed him to finally accept that the only person to blame that night had been his father, and that it was time for him to let go at last. He'd spent nearly two decades focusing on his army life, his career, throwing himself into it as a way to avoid having to consider what his non-army life had been like. He'd thrown up a wall between his personal life and his professional one, always keeping himself on the side of the latter. But in a matter of months Elle had begun to take down that wall, brick by brick, and now he knew that he could step over what was left of that division if he wanted to. He could finally consider a future that didn't centre on his career. Fitz wasn't yet sure what that future might hold, he only knew it contained Elle.

He just had to convince her of that.

But he could wait. A day, a week, a month, until they had the chance to be alone again. She deserved to know how very incredible, and special, and unique she was. How he couldn't foresee a life without her in it. And how what they had wasn't transitory or a bit of fun, because she was the only woman with whom he could ever—*had* ever—been able to see tantalising glimpses of a future.

Unexpectedly, Elle turned, although he hadn't said a word, and even if he had she could never have heard him over the clamour. It was an instinct that had begun to bind them ever since that first night.

'Colonel?'

He couldn't hear the words but he could read her lips, and still it didn't stop him from speaking aloud, the words swallowed up within the pandemonium, yet that did nothing to diminish the excitement bubbling inside him.

Like he was once again the kid he'd stopped being the night he'd lost his beloved mother.

'Nothing.' He smiled. 'Everything.'

For a moment Elle simply stared, as though trying to be sure that he meant what she thought. And then she responded with a smile of her own, the bright, easy, open Elle-style beam shining as brightly, as warmly as if she could reflect the very sun from the sky.

His Elle. He could spend the rest of his life bathed in the glow of her happiness and be a contented man. And he would willingly spend the rest of his life making sure she felt every bit as treasured, as admired, as loved as she deserved.

CHAPTER FOURTEEN

ANOTHER CHEER WENT up as they finally freed yet another kid from the rubble. Dirty and exhausted but most certainly alive. He lifted the tiny body as the child clung madly to him, his eyes locked on an exhausted Elle as she hurried over to them.

'Bring her this way, we've set up more treatment areas over here…' She indicated. 'And then you need to take a break. When is the last time you ate?'

'When's the last time *you* did?' Fitz challenged, following her as she lifted the rope to the cordoned-off area that allowed her to triage and treat without the pressure of understandably desperate relatives crowding in to see proof for themselves of their missing loved one.

As they slipped inside the tents the little girl was whisked away by Elle's team, what looked to be her mother crying with relief by a waiting bed.

It had been almost twenty hours since they'd started securing the area and finding people to pull free. Even now, they were still finding occasional survivors, the shouts for silence going up any time they thought they heard sounds of a survivor, and marvelling at the resilience of the human spirit. But the death toll, low in the first few hours, was now beginning to race up, the bodies more damaged the deeper they excavated, and Fitz knew he would have to put the local volunteers on three-hour maximums before making them take a compulsory break, and to talk to someone about what they'd seen. His own men could work longer shifts, but it was still back-breaking work that was becoming increasingly demoralising the more time passed and the fewer survivors they found.

'I've just had a break, actually,' Elle said gently, answering his original question.

'Voluntarily?' he couldn't quite picture that. 'You mean someone *made* you take a break.'

Her sheepish expression said it all.

'The point is that you need to stop and eat, regroup,' she admonished anyway.

No one was around to overhear but, still, they both knew it was their way of silently showing each other they cared. In spite of their surroundings, he couldn't help an unexpected wisp of happiness from curling up inside him.

'I will when relief arrives,' he consented eventually.

She glanced up quickly.

'It should have arrived about half an hour ago. Major Howes brought his other two troops and Major Richards brought his squadron.'

'But they haven't reached us?'

'No.'

Fitz frowned.

'Which means it's likely there's been another slide on the other side of the valley, on the way in. I have to go and find out.'

'No,' Elle commanded, stepping inside. 'I'll give this little girl a check-up and then I want to inspect those stitches of yours, to see if they're still holding up. I'm surprised you haven't burst them out there.'

'Is that a medical order, Major?' Fitz cocked his eyebrow.

'It is.' She smiled, ducking into the next tent to retrieve a few medical supplies.

He settled on the edge of the bed, ready to expose the dressing on his shoulder.

'Fitz?'

He stiffened, turned.

It couldn't be.

'Janine?'

He steeled himself for the inevitable guilt but it didn't come.

Instead, in that instant, he finally understood what had happened with Janine. It had barely been a couple of years since the car crash and he'd been so desperate to fix the yearning chasm in his soul after his family's deaths that he'd seen the way this sweet, young girl had loved him and he'd tried to convince himself that if he could love her back then he wouldn't be damaged any more. He wouldn't be alone any more. But Janine, as gentle as she was, could never have helped him rebuild his shattered past enough to move on. Janine would always have needed someone whole, untainted by tragedy, someone *she* could lean on to escape her controlling father. She could never have seen or understood the twisted mess inside him, much less helped him to untangle it. He would always have provided for their baby but in many ways it was a good thing there had never been a child stuck in the middle of them. He would always have been the wrong man for Janine, just as she could never have been the right woman for him. She wasn't Elle.

'Thank God you're here.' She exhaled heavily.

Abruptly, Fitz registered Janine's blanched, pre-occupied expression and he forgot all his insignificant personal demons.

'I didn't know your logistics unit was out here.'

'We were bringing the generators through the valley to a new hospital being built when a small slide hit multiple vehicles in the middle of our convoy,' she stated.

'Everyone okay?'

'Mostly, a couple of four-by-fours rolled and there are some bumps and bruises but we got lucky. Fortunately none of the gennies were hit.'

'There should be a couple of my squadrons out there now.' He frowned as Janine nodded.

'They were behind us, they're clearing and securing the area now. They've got better equipment for it and we had to keep going as we have a time constraint for getting the generators to the hospital. There's an MRI coming on our next run.'

It wasn't just the MRI. Fitz thought of the last ancient back-up generator they'd repaired too many times already. It was imperative they get the new generators to the site because if the back-up failed before the new generators were in place, the hospital would have no power at all.

'If Major Howes is dealing with the landslide

then you're going to need me to head to the hospital with you,' he decided quickly.

'Major Howes assured me he'd be right behind us.'

'No.' Fitz quickly ran through the route in his head. 'There's a bridge between here and the hospital, we already recced it but that was before the earthquake. I want to make sure it hasn't been weakened and won't collapse under the weight of those gennies.'

Her relief was obvious.

'Thank you.'

He was off the bed and across the tent before Elle's voice, tight and high, halted him.

'Colonel, your arm.'

He turned to see her standing at the back of the tent, supplies in hand, her expression stricken. She'd obviously heard most of the conversation.

Fitz hesitated for a fraction of a second. He wanted to tell her, to explain to her that, as much as he would be doing this anyway to complete a crucial mission, there was also a personal element to it now. Because in helping Janine he felt as though he would finally get closure on his regret from their past. And if he did, then he would finally have a clear conscience. He could at last be free to look to a new, more promising future with Elle. He wanted to tell her all of that, but there was no time. Instead, he invested every bit of meaning he could into his words, hoping she'd understand the message.

'You need to be checked out. Major Caplin will do it. I'll get a team together.'

He also needed to get Carl to bring at least one of the troops to the valley to join the rescue effort here.

'I really *do* need to check that wound, Colonel,' Elle asserted firmly, but he waved her away.

The sooner he completed this mission, the sooner he could consider a future with her.

'Major Caplin, my arm's fine. I have to leave now. Please check over Major Billings here. Pack up your kit and your team and head out as soon as you're ready. Don't wait for me.'

The expression on her face twisted his gut. He'd hurt her. Again. And he couldn't do a thing about it. He would have to be content with seeing her back at the hospital. Then they could finally have a conversation that he now realised was long overdue. Unless she ran, like he suspected she might.

And if she did, then he would have no choice but to respect her decision. He would have to let her go.

Don't wait for me.

Elle stared at the heavy-duty canvas tent flap long after Fitz had disappeared and it had dropped heavily back into place. There was no doubt in her mind that Fitz had been trying to tell her something. A message within the words.

She forced herself to turn to the major, dredging up her practised medical smile. She couldn't shake the feeling the woman was watching her shrewdly. Yet another of Fitz's admirers, no doubt.

'Can you sit on the bed, please, Major Billings?'

'Janine,' the woman introduced herself immediately.

Janine.

It hit Elle like a blast wave. Suddenly it all made sense.

Janine.

Fitz was still in love with her.

He'd chosen her over Elle's own medical advice. And, Elle couldn't help feeling, he'd chosen Janine over her personally. She was second again. Dispensable. Just like she'd been to Stevie. Only the difference here was that Fitz had never broken any commitment to her because he'd never of-fered her any promises. From the outset he'd told her that they didn't have a future, that he didn't *do* relationships.

The error had been on her part in allowing herself to believe that he didn't do relationships because he hadn't yet met the right person, the woman who could help him to get past the trauma and guilt of his past. And the error had been in thinking that she could be that woman and ignoring what had been right under her nose. That Janine had always been in the forefront of Fitz's head.

Don't wait for me.

As painful and unbearable as it might be, she had to listen to him. Fitz didn't want her. He'd made that clear again and again, she'd just cho-sen to read something more into it. She'd chosen to believe it was because he couldn't find a way to open up to her, and she'd chosen to believe that if she loved him enough she could find a way to help him.

She'd been wrong. She would pack up here and finish up the last few days in Razorwire before returning home. The hospital didn't need her, the next squadron was out here already and the relief teams had taken over.

She wouldn't come back as long as Fitz was still out here. She couldn't bear to work alongside him, loving him but unable to do a thing about it.

'You know who I am,' Janine said slowly, her eyes watching Elle intently.

She could play it down the line, strictly professional, of course. But they were both grown women, both majors, both equals.

'I know a little,' Elle hedged.

To her surprise, Janine's shoulders sagged and the woman looked defeated.

'So he really is in love with you.'

It was more a comment to herself than to Elle, but still Elle couldn't help snorting with nervous shock.

'You couldn't be more wrong.'

Sharp eyes pierced Elle as Janine jerked her head up.

'You didn't know?'

Elle focussed on her job, unsure what else to say.

'I sensed something between you the moment he saw you come in.' Janine spoke softly, almost wistfully. 'I would have given anything for him to look at me, just once, the way he looked at you at that moment.'

Elle told herself not to listen, not to believe, not

to let that little flicker of hope surge so strongly inside her. She told herself it would only hurt all the more when she had to prove Janine was wrong.

And still the hope grew, leaning towards Janine's words the way a tree leaned to the sun. Making her admit things she would never have admitted to anyone, least of all Janine.

'It isn't love. At least, not on Fitz's part.' The words spilled out before she could stop herself.

But instead of Janine using the confession as ammunition, as Elle might have feared, the woman simply offered a sweet, if watery smile.

'Did he tell you about the baby?'

Elle didn't know how to answer.

'He did.' Janine nodded, as if she'd suspected as much. 'Then you're wrong. He loves you very much. I don't think he's ever told anyone about me. About us, such as there ever was an us.'

'He didn't go into detail,' Elle found herself half-apologising, as though she was intruding on someone else's business.

'That sounds like Fitz.' Janine offered another soft, sad smile. 'But the fact that he opened up to you at all should tell you all you need to know about how much he values you. How about his family? Did he tell you about them?'

She should end the conversation. It felt disloyal talking about Fitz behind his back. But a part of her couldn't stop. He'd told her she was the only person he'd ever wanted to talk to about his family. At the time it had made her feel special, valued, as though he wanted her to understand him in a way he never had with anyone else.

It had turned out that was just a lie.

'I know his mother and sister died in the car crash,' Elle said after a moment.

Janine frowned.

'It was his whole family. His poor father, too. It must have been devastating for Fitz, losing his whole family in one single instant, but he never spoke about it.'

Elle hesitated. Didn't Janine know his father had been drinking? Had reappeared out of nowhere? Had abused his mother?

'But he spoke about it with you,' she pointed out cautiously, deliberately focussing on the check-up and avoiding Janine's direct gaze.

'Only because I made him. My father…he was a colonel back then, and when he found out that I'd been pregnant he told me to forget about Fitz, about the car crash. Told me that he was damaged.'

Damaged.

Exactly the words Fitz had used to describe himself that first night.

'Did you ever say that to him?' she demanded, unable to help herself. 'Did you ever tell him he was damaged?'

The woman dropped her head, misery and guilt etched in every crevice and curve.

'I never should have, I know that. But I was hurt and I was grieving. I'd just lost my baby, and Fitz didn't seem bothered. I know now he was probably still numb from finding out in the first place—I'd only told him I was pregnant a few hours earlier...'

'A few hours?' Elle exclaimed.

'He didn't tell you that?'

'He told me you were three months pregnant when you went out on that convoy. That he didn't stop you. That he should have told someone and made sure you were sent home to safety. He holds himself responsible.'

'Fitz does?' Janine twisted around to face Elle. 'How could any of it be his fault? I only told him that morning, before the convoy went out. I knew he was in shock but he immediately told me we'd get married and he would take care of us, just as I'd known he would. My convoy was due back that night and then I was heading home for R&R. I was going to tell my parents then.'

'He never said.' Elle shook her head.

Part of her was still reeling, yet another part of her was absorbing the revelations, sifting them in with the story Fitz had told her, working through how it had impacted on him. Compounding the guilt and helplessness and vulnerability he must already have felt at losing his mother and sister only a few years earlier.

No wonder he had trust issues.

No wonder he found it hard to let her in.

If she really loved him as much as she thought she did, then she had to find a way to prove she wasn't going to let him down or leave him, while giving him the time and space he needed to accept her.

'He thinks he let you down, betrayed your trust,' Elle said at length.

It was a risk, telling Janine something that Fitz had told her in confidence, but Elle decided it was a risk she was prepared to take. Despite everything, there was a part of her that couldn't help liking Janine and feeling sorry for her. She was no doubt a decent enough major, her army father would have drilled that into her, but as a woman

Janine seemed a little naïve, a bit young for her age. And yet if anyone could tell her the truth about Fitz, Elle couldn't help feeling it was going to be this woman.

'He never let me down.' Janine hung her head again. 'I let *him* down. I…manipulated him. I'm not proud of it. But I was twenty-two and I was naïve and foolish, and I was desperate to get away from my controlling father. I fell for Fitz the first week of our officer training course, he was different from the other lads. Stronger, more focussed, resolute.

'The longer I spent in his company, the more I fell in love. I thought if I could give him a family—like the one he'd lost—then I could break through those barriers of his and he would love me back. But he never did. He would have married me, he would have taken care of me, of our baby. But he never loved me like I thought I loved him. Yet if I *had* loved him, I suppose I never would have wanted to trap him.'

'Getting pregnant was deliberate?' Elle managed slowly.

'*No!* At least, I don't think so. Maybe. No. I don't know, subconsciously perhaps? And I regret it, more than you can imagine.'

'Why tell me all this?' Elle asked, her curiosity finally getting the better of her.

Janine shrugged.

'I'm not sure. Guilt, I suppose. I've been carrying it around with me all this time, wondering how Fitz is doing. I followed his career for a while but I knew he had a reputation for never getting involved with anyone. Then I stopped. I realised I wasn't doing myself any favours refusing to let go of the past. When I saw you in here, I don't know… I guess I thought it was my chance to make amends.'

'Ironic,' Elle mused softly.

'What is?'

Elle hesitated, wondering whether it was wise to say anything else, then deciding that it was the least she could do after Janine had been so painfully honest with her.

'I could be wrong, but I have a feeling Fitz wanting to be the one to personally take charge of this mission and accompany your convoy is as much about making amends to you and ensuring your safety as it is about ensuring the generator's safety. Maybe he feels he owes you, maybe it's about closure.'

'He doesn't owe me anything,' Janine answered

quietly. 'But I'll happily take the closure. So what about you? What are you going to do now?'

Elle was spared any response as a young corporal appeared at the tent door, breathing hard from running.

'Major Billings, Colonel Fitzwilliam told me to inform you that his vehicle is ready when your convoy is cleared to go.'

'Understood.' Janine nodded, turning to Elle as she slid off the bed. 'Am I clear to leave?'

'You seem fine,' confirmed Elle.

'Okay, well…as to the other thing, good luck.'

Elle watched as the woman hurried away. The silence only emphasised the way her heart was beating out a tattoo and the blood was rushing in her ears.

Fitz was just as damaged as he'd tried to tell her, but she hadn't listened. She hadn't really understood. Now she knew more, and she understood better. If she crowded Fitz then she was only going to compound the issue. Especially when her own insecurities were still so close to the surface. She hadn't realised, until she'd seen Fitz and Janine in that first instant and had felt that surge of jealousy that had been so absent when she'd walked in on Stevie, that she'd never allowed herself to heal.

Not just from the obvious pain of being cheated on by her fiancé, but because she'd never allowed herself to mourn the boy who had saved her from the misery of her teenage years as he'd turned into a man she hadn't recognised. Hadn't even liked.

Until she allowed herself to repair a decade of a mentally draining relationship, how could she possibly dive into another one with Fitz? They both needed time to heal, to work out who they were, to go into any new relationship without unnecessary baggage from their respective pasts.

But a tiny part of her was terrified to leave things as they were with Fitz. Because if she walked away, he could close the door on her that final inch and she'd never be able to get back in.

She had absolutely no idea what to do.

CHAPTER FIFTEEN

FITZ TOOK OUT the piece of paper for the hundredth time since he'd found Elle's address and jotted it down.

He didn't think he'd ever forget the despair that had scraped at his insides when he'd discovered she'd spent her last few days at Razorwire and had left without a word.

As though he'd meant nothing.

As though they'd meant nothing.

He'd sworn to himself that he wouldn't follow her. That if she walked away he would let her go. But it had felt so different when it had actually happened.

He'd thrown himself back into his work, into the mission, but at every turn he had been reminded of Elle. Brigade had been more than pleased with the progress they'd already made on the hospital and he'd been forced to remember that much of it had been down to Elle's expertise on the layout, her ability to communicate the hospital's needs, and her capacity for compromise with the engineering priorities. The fact that they had clicked so easily together, working as such a good team, only made it all the harder to push aside the memories of her.

The day he'd received the details of his R&R flight home, he'd known he had to find Elle. To speak to her. To convince her that they should at least try to see if there wasn't some future for them.

And now he was minutes from landing, and it was time to decide whether to bin the address and let her get on with her life, or visit in the hope of… what? Convincing her to try a relationship with a man who didn't have the faintest idea of how a real one should work? A man who was more than likely going to hurt her despite his best intentions because, when it came to love, his best wouldn't be enough?

Fitz closed his eyes and waited for the plane to begin its final descent, the weight of hope, expectation and uncertainly all pressing down more intensely on his shoulders than even the heaviest of military packs. When the plane finally landed, he still had no idea what he should do. Losing her from his life had been unbearable even for the short time since she'd finished her tour of duty, but convincing her to risk more of herself only to lose her permanently, and no doubt crush her in the process, was unconscionable.

He was still coming to terms with what Janine had told him this last time they'd met.

Fitz was still lost in his thoughts as he split off from the soldiers heading out of the front door for the coaches, and instead strode out of the side door of the hangar, which led to the senior officers' parking area. And then he saw her in front of him, resting, in civvy clothes that reminded with startling clarity of that first night, on the bonnet of her car.

He stopped dead, then slowly, very slowly managed to instruct his legs to work again as he walked up to her.

'Major.'

'Colonel.'

That slight quirk of her mouth tugged at his chest.

'Elle.'

'Fitz.'

She walked around to the driver's door, letting herself in and clipping her seatbelt on. When he still hadn't moved, she lowered the window.

'Are you getting in or not?'

So calm, and cool, as though she knew exactly what she was doing and wasn't plagued by even one of the doubts that collided inside his head. She made him want to believe it would all be okay. She made him want to see himself through her eyes.

She made him want to be the man she saw through her eyes.

The piece of paper with her address on it fluttered in the breeze, still held in his fingers. He smiled wryly and passed it through the window to her before opening the boot and putting his pack in. By the time he slid into the passenger seat, she had already started the engine.

'So,' she asked a few minutes later as she pulled away from the gatehouse and onto the main road, 'were you going to use it?'

'Your address? I honestly don't know,' he answered. 'I kept telling myself to be a better man and let you go, but I suspect I couldn't have stayed away for the entire two weeks.'

She didn't answer at first, then she dipped her head in a simple nod.

'Good.'

He let her drive, watching out of the window thoughtfully. It was only when she pulled up in a quiet road and he saw the house numbers that he realised they matched the address on the paper. She'd brought him to her home.

It gave him an irrational surge of satisfaction.

Her smile was like a beacon of light as she unclipped her seatbelt and, wordlessly, he followed her into her house. He couldn't help taking everything in, from the muted, sophisticated colour scheme on the walls and floor to the vibrant splashes of colour in fun paintings or soft furnishings. It was all so essentially Elle. Every last photograph, every last knick-knack—not that there were many of either—but the selective few only emphasised her personality all the more. Her home reflected every different facet of her personality, solid and consistent yet quirky and dynamic.

Oddly, it felt like the closest thing to a home he'd ever known, and he'd barely been here for a few minutes.

It only made him want to be with her all the more.

'About Janine—' he began, but Elle silenced him.

'I don't want to know about your past. At least, not right now. You still have stuff to work through and, since I thought about it, so do I. I've already told you that you can't underestimate guilt, Fitz. Believe me, I know how complicated and confusing it can be. But what I want to know is if you want us to work through it together. I want to know if you see a future for us.'

'I don't know *how* to build a future with someone—my whole adult life all I've ever concentrated on is my career, or it was until you came along—but I want to try. For the record, I never said it back that day but I know I love you. I just don't know if love is enough.'

'That's still a great start.' Her breath whooshed out as she took a step towards him.

'But is it enough?'

'Who knows? It will be if we want it to be. It will depend on us, I guess.'

He wanted to believe as she did. More than anything.

'And if it falls apart?' He barely recognised the strangled voice as his, echoing all the fears in his soul. 'If I can't be the man you need, the man you deserve, if it's not in my DNA?'

'I told you, let go of your past.' She took that final step.

Her toes pushed against his, her breath rippled over the skin in the small V of his chest, where his shirt was unbuttoned. Then higher, as she tilted her head to look at him.

'What happens if I hurt you?'

She took his face in her hands and he felt every last inch of that old, familiar, unwelcome glacier in his chest crack and slide away.

'And what happens if you don't?' she whispered.

His hands came up to hold hers, then hauled her to him. Elle had no idea how long they stood entwined, as though he never wanted to let her go. She only knew she didn't want to move, didn't even want to breathe heavily in case it shattered the perfect moment.

Her little home suddenly felt more alive than she'd ever known it. Fitz filled the space, the air crackling around them, and it felt like the place could barely contain him. Or maybe it could barely contain all that flowed between them. She'd always hated anyone in her home. It had always been her sanctuary, her personal space from the world. Her real life away from the ever-increasing opulence of Stevie's luxury bachelor pads. This had been *her* perfect home, and only her best friend Fliss had ever been welcome.

And now Fitz.

Somehow it felt as though he'd always belonged here.

'I want to promise you everything,' he murmured into her hair, his hand cupping her head like she was the most precious thing in the world to him. 'You make me feel things I never knew existed before. Like what I thought was important isn't as significant any more, and yet things I never gave a second thought to are suddenly vital. Like anything is possible as long as you are by my side.'

He shook his head, still trying to fathom it.

'You make me feel cherished,' she added simply.

Her words humbled him and yet made his chest swell with pride all at once.

'But we've both said in the past that words mean nothing without actions to back them up.'

'So don't say them,' she whispered. 'You've already told me you love me, and that's enough for now. We'll work on the rest through actions, deal?'

'Agreed. But for the record, can I tell you one thing again?' His voice rumbled low against her cheek now, and she shivered in anticipation. 'Because I don't ever want to tire of saying it. I love you, Major Gabriella Caplin.'

'I love you too.' She drew her head back, her

smile freezing on her lips, her breath catching in her throat.

She didn't want to talk any more. She wanted something else entirely. Fitz's eyes were dark, intense, hungry. But there was something else, too. Something more. Promises he couldn't yet articulate and she wasn't ready to hear. Like they'd agreed. Actions. Not words.

'Enough talking,' he muttered abruptly, bringing his mouth down to claim hers with a fire she hoped would never be quenched. He kissed her with all the unspoken words that lay between them. He kissed her with all the possession she needed to make her feel wanted. He kissed her with all his flawed yet perfect heart.

And when he finally, reluctantly pulled away, she felt strangely bereft. Just like that first night.

'There was one other thing I brought,' he said suddenly. 'Wait here.'

She watched as he slid the keys from the basket on her hall stand and dashed out to the car. And then he was back and the palm-sized pretty velvet box in his hands made her stomach flip-flop. A tiny bit of excitement, a lot of fear, but mainly with disappointment.

Because he didn't know her at all after all. She wasn't ready for this yet. It wasn't right.

'When did you do this?' she asked nervously, hoping he couldn't tell she was stalling.

'In Razorwire. It's where I got the box. It's odd the things some people send in care packages.'

He was edgy too, she realised. But it didn't help. She licked her lips.

'Fitz, this is—'

'Just open it, Elle,' he insisted quietly.

Heavy-hearted, she pulled at the bow with painstaking hesitation and clicked open the box.

Her entire body soared until her head felt dizzy.

'It's a key!' she exclaimed.

He'd remembered and this was his way of showing her—proving to her—that she could trust him. The first of his actions-not-words promise. Her grin was so wide it was almost uncomfortable. *Had she ever known how it felt to be this happy?*

'To my place,' confirmed Fitz. 'You can call in whenever you want. No invitation necessary.'

'Thank you.' Her voice cracked as she nodded vigorously. 'It's perfect.'

'Like you,' he murmured, pulling her back into his arms. 'Now, where were we?'

* * *

Elle could hear the Gurkha piper playing as she and Fitz turned. The honour guard formed outside the doors of the church, fellow officers from both their regiments only too happy to play their part in the big day.

'Happy?' Fitz murmured as they began their walk down the aisle, permanent grins attached to both their faces.

'It doesn't even begin to describe it.' The laughter bubbled up inside her. 'The perfect culmination to a wonderful three years together.'

'It gets better,' a voice chirped up from behind as Elle swung around to grin at Fliss, her heavily pregnant matron of honour.

'If your waters break on my wedding dress train,' Elle teased in a threatening voice, 'well… I won't mind a bit. I'm just relieved you made it through the service.'

And then Fliss disappeared into the background as Fitz wrapped his arm around her—her new husband. It felt so exciting and yet so fitting.

'Come on, Major Fitzwilliam.' Fitz chuckled. 'Or are you sticking with Major Caplin?'

'You already know the answer.' She swatted him gently even as he led her out of the church doors and under the honour guard. 'Definitely Fitzwilliam, but they'd better not call me Fitz.'

'They wouldn't dare. Not the incoming lieutenant colonel of the field hospital, and an OBE to boot.'

He soundest almost prouder of her than she was herself. But, then, that was Fitz. In the last three years he'd never let her down, never put his career ahead of hers. They'd worked together, well and truly buried any last demons, and now they were beginning another new, pristine chapter of their lives together. And Elle couldn't wait.

'Well, I had to do something to keep up with you, Deputy Assistant Chief of Staff for HQ Telridge Command. Although thanks to your new post, starting tomorrow morning, this is going to be the shortest honeymoon in history.'

'I'll make it up to you,' Fitz promised.

'No need.' She turned to him as his arm snaked about her back and he pulled her close. 'Enough talking, more action, soldier.'

And he obliged. As he always did.

* * * * *